Contents

Key

71–74 / 71–74 cross-reference between playscript and teaching resources.

H in resources = activity suitable for homework.

Characters

A Woman Doctor

Jonathan Harker a solicitor

Seward the owner of a psychiatric hospital

Renfield a patient in the psychiatric hospital

Wilhelmina Murray (Mina) Harker's fiancée, later wife

Dracula a Transylvanian Count

Attendant/Vampire One attendant in the hospital/ beautiful female vampire

Attendant/Vampire Two attendant in the hospital/ beautiful female vampire

Fair girl a beautiful female vampire

Quincey Morris a rich American

Lord Godalming an English aristocrat, Lucy's fiancé

Abraham Van Helsing a famous physician

Lucy Westenra a young Englishwoman

Lucy Westenra's mother

Dracula

by

Bram Stoker

Adapted by
Jan Needle

Resource Material by
Viv Gardner

Series Consultant
Stephen Cockett

Published by HarperCollins *Publishers* Limited, 77–85 Fulham Palace Road, Hammersmith, London W6 8JB

First published 2000

12

ISBN-13 978 0 00 330224 0
ISBN-10 0 00 330224 5

British Library Cataloguing in Publication Data

A catalogue record for this publication is available from the British Library.

Commissioned by Helen Clark, edited by Domenica de Rosa, Toby Satterthwaite and Rachel Normington, picture research by Charles Evans
Design by Nigel Jordan, cover design by Nigel Jordan, cover illustration by Zhenya Matysiak

Acknowledgements
The following permissions to reproduce material are gratefully acknowledged: Nigel Jordan, p67; © Topham Picturepoint, p71; © Hulton Getty, p73; © The Ronald Grant Archive, p74; © The Board of Trustees of the Victoria & Albert Museum, p75; © Colindale, p76; *Varney the Vampire or the Feast of Blood*, 1846, is taken from the 'Penny Dreadful' Series, p86; Count Duckula is reproduced with permission of Pearson Television Stills Library, p86; 'Buffy the Vampire Slayer' extract, taken from *Uninvited Guests*, is reproduced with permission of T M & copyright Twentieth Century Fox Film Coorporation. All rights reserved, pp87–8.

Whilst every effort has been made both to contact the copyright holders and to give exact credit lines, this has not proved possible in every case.

Printed by RR Donnelley at Glasgow, UK.

For permission to perform this play, please allow plenty of time and contact: Permissions Department, HarperCollins *Publishers*, 77–85 Fulham Palace Road, London W6 8JB. Tel. 020 8741 7070

Dracula

Scene One

__Seward__ is at the table, with a young __woman doctor__ in a chair opposite. To one side are two female __attendants__, silent and demure. On the couch, flat out, is __Harker__, apparently asleep. Beyond it, __Renfield's__ head is visible. He is seated, leaning against the couch.

69

Woman So let's run through it one more time, Dr Seward. Before he wakes. Six years ago? Correct?

Seward Seven. The whole thing blew up in 1897. November 6. Not bad timing, for such an explosive happening.

Woman I'm afraid I don't follow you.

Seward November 6. The day after Guy Fawkes. When the rockets ... oh, never mind.

Woman And our clients for today were how old?

Seward Seven years ago? Jonathan Harker was twenty-seven, Mina not quite nineteen.

Woman Mina Murray?

Seward No, no, Mina Harker, they were married by this time. Mina went to Budapest to rescue him from a convent, and they married. *(Brief laugh)* When I say *rescued* from a convent ...

Woman You don't mean the nuns were on the rampage. No, I've grasped that much. He had gone into the Balkans, to Transylvania, and had some sort of breakdown. He'd gone there as an estate agent, is that correct?

Seward No, that's what Mina says, in her more acid moments. She can be very acid, with Jonathan. In fact he was a solicitor, sent by his firm in Exeter to close a deal. The property was in England, the would-be buyer was a nobleman. Count Dracula.

Woman *(checks notes)* Count Dracula. Ah yes, it is all here. And Mr Harker had a breakdown. According to your notes he had amazing dreams, erotic nightmares, wild women coming to his castle room at midnight. What brought on these odd delusions?

Seward Delusions. Well, so you say. But Abraham Van Helsing, when I called him all the way from Amsterdam, was of a very different view. I trust you would not discount him in this? He is the world authority.

Woman I would not dream of it. Abraham Van Helsing's knowledge of such strange matters is quite unparalleled.

Seward His efforts were heroic, I can tell you. He gave his all. He almost gave his life. I assure you, doctor, the possibility that this was delusion did not come into it. Van Helsing was entirely convinced.

Woman Well, then. I hope that I might question him about it, later. You must forgive my scepticism until then, Dr Seward. Seductive maidens who throw themselves upon men in mountain castles are outside my day-to-day experience. The stuff of fantasy, a New Woman might say. The stuff of dreams.

Seward These were the stuff of nightmares. They came to suck young Mr Harker's blood. *(Calls)* Renfield! Is he awake yet? I think you'd better wake him up, don't you?

Renfield *gets to his feet and shambles into view. He trails a straitjacket like a child's comfort blanket. He pokes at* ***Harker****, who jumps.*

Renfield Come on, young sir! Wakey wakey!

Woman He seems very sluggish.

Seward He sleeps a lot. They all do, those that survived. It was a terrible ordeal, doctor. Two died, you know. Quincey Morris at the hands of Dracula, and Lucy Westenra –

Renfield – at his teeth! Oh, very neat that, Dr Seward. Fangs for the memory, eh?!

Harker Shut up, Renfield, you awful oaf. Where is my wife?

Seward Yes, go and get her, Renfield. The doctor here has trouble understanding. She must hear this awful story from all sides.

***Renfield** opens a small tin box and proffers it to **Harker**.*

Renfield Would you like a spider or a fly for while you're waiting? I've got some lovely bluebottles.

Harker You're completely mad!

Renfield *(leaving)* You don't have to be to work here, so they say! But it sure as goodness helps!

***Harker** pulls a pillow over his face and lies there.*

Woman This is fascinating, Doctor Seward. Are they all so seriously disturbed?

Seward When they got back, the Harkers' lives and psyches were already wrecked, I think. And Mina's friend, Miss Westenra, was ... At only eighteen years. So young, so rich ...

Harker So dead. She was the one who first called me an estate agent, she put Mina up to it. No better than she should have been, in my opinion.

Woman I beg your pardon, Mr Harker. I didn't catch that.

Harker *(removes pillow for a second)* I don't want to talk.

Woman Then I must talk to Doctor Seward. You must listen. *(Checks notes)* You are Jonathan Harker, I believe, aged thirty-four. Normal residence Exeter, in Devon. Profession, solicitor.

Harker *(lifts pillow)* Not an estate agent.

Woman Some years ago, in '97, you went to Eastern Europe to negotiate with one Count Dracula for the purchase of a property not far from here called ... er ... Carstairs.

Seward Carfax. Not very far indeed; next door, in fact. An ancient pile later incorporated into this ...

Harker Lunatic asylum.

Woman Clinic.

Seward Nursing home.

Woman Where Mr Harker is a private patient.

Harker Guest.

Seward Definitely a guest. We've been friends for years. He's as sane as I am, what!

Woman But, somehow or another, this simple business trip became more complicated.

Harker It became a nightmare! He was a monster. A demon. His purpose, Madam Doctor, was to destroy the world!

Seward And poor Jonathan ... we are all agreed on this, Jonathan, no shame attached, at all ... poor Jonathan suffered some sort of massive brain collapse.

Woman I understand. That whole area, Mr Harker – the Carpathians, the Balkan heart of Mittel Europe, call it what you will – to Western eyes and ears and brains it *is* a nightmare, isn't it? Serbia, Croatia, Moldavia, Bosnia, Kosovo – they have fought and killed each other for a thousand years. It is the most hate-filled portion of our modern world.

Harker Hate is the word. Count Dracula classed hate as his life-force, it was glowing in his eyes. In his small state alone, in Transylvania, he told me there were four distinct racial groups, all descended from Attila*, all vying to out-Hun that worst of Huns*! He boasted that every square foot of his native soil was soaked in blood, in Turkish blood, and Czech, Hungarian, Slovak, Slav and Dacian. When I suggested that the hate must surely one day end, Count Dracula...

Woman Yes?

Harker He laughed.

Seward *(to **Woman**)* He did not often laugh. That is significant.

---

* King of the Huns, circa AD 406–53

* a warlike Asiatic people who invaded Europe in the 4th–5th centuries

Harker *(emotional)* He did not *ever* laugh! His lips were thin, his hands were cold as ice, he had a cruel, *cruel* mouth. He ... *did ... not ... laugh*!

Woman *(unimpressed)* You say 'cruel'. A subjective judgement, surely?

Seward Doctor, this was a man alone. He was trapped, virtually a prisoner, in that land of ancient hatreds.

Harker I *was* alone. A captive! In a place bereft* of pity!

Woman *(to Seward)* An emotional sort of man? Prone to melodrama?

Seward *(stiffly)* I did not know him then but I sincerely doubt it. I only came to know him through his wife, who was a friend of poor dear Lucy Westenra.

Harker *(bitterly)* 'Dear' Lucy. Oh yes, indeed. They were courting her, doctor, all three of them, has Dr Seward told you that? They were flies around that little honey pot, Mina told me so. Her band of would-be lovers! Seward, Godalming and Quincey Morris. Then she died. *I* never had the pleasure.

Seward *(sternly)* Jonathan, you must hush. You do not help sometimes. Lucy died because of Dracula, and when he turned his sights on Wilhelmina, you fought him to the death. When I first met him, doctor, this man's hair was black. It turned to silver almost overnight. In the Balkans, you must understand it, he was alone.

Harker *(contrite)* Forgive me, Jack, my self-control is truly lamentable. Madam, Jack Seward and my other friends – Lord Godalming, Van Helsing, poor dead Quincey Morris – they were lions in the fight. They were towers of strength to me. In Castle Dracula I *was* alone. When I escaped I barely had my sanity. Those good nuns, then Mina, saved my life.

Woman Perhaps you'd better try to tell me details. That would help. How did you get there? What did you find?

---

* without

HARKER Oh God, it was beyond belief. A freezing, lonely journey to a castle on a pinnacle of rock, a cold, bare mountain top. No servants, footmen, grooms, housekeeper, cook, or anyone. And as he served me food – alone, the count touched not a morsel or a drop – I noticed that his hands were terrible. They were broad, squat-fingered, with nails cut into long sharp points. His breath was rank; cold and reeking as an open tomb. It almost made me gag.

WOMAN This is *very* interesting. *(Taking notes very seriously)* The detail is of great morbidity*, almost transcendental*. But – well; you say some sort of demon, or a monster? You don't mean *literally*, do you? He was a house-buyer. Looking for a home in Surrey.

HARKER Oh *please*. Jack, *tell* her.

WOMAN He called you into Mittel Europe, a thousand miles and more from England, then tried to – to *what*, precisely? Kill you? Are you serious?

HARKER *(desperate)* How dare you doubt me! I am a man of law! Why will you not believe my evidence?

WOMAN Because it's unbelievable! *(She scatters notes, seeking)* Here, for instance! Here, where is it? You state his age as six hundred-and-forty-seven. Just like that! It is, at best ...

SEWARD *(smoothly)* Unusual. But in the Balkans, you must agree ...

WOMAN And this count! This nobleman! He has no cook, he does not eat and drink, and yet he serves up food and has bad breath! That, surely Dr Seward, indicates digestive problems? Of course he eats! It does not agree with him! They call it indigestion!

HARKER *(shrieks)* They call it human blood! He drank it! He drank Lucy Westenra's! He drank my wife's! That was his sustenance! Blood!

WOMAN *(soberly)* I am here to help, not to be shouted at. We have got to talk this through. This *is* a lunati ...

SEWARD A nursing home.

---

* unpleasantness

* beyond experience

Harker *(contritely)* And I *was* mad in Transylvania, I grant you. Even after I escaped his demon clutches and was nursed to normal life by those good nuns. When Mina came to bring me home, I was still indeed near death. But I'm not mad now, I'm sane. However strange it seems, my story is the plain, unvarnished truth. Where's Mina? What is Renfield doing? Where is my dear wife? She'll tell you.

Woman *(craftily)* Are you so sure she will? Doctor Seward called her 'acid'. *(With sudden harshness)* Why did you marry her, Mr Harker?

Seward Doctor, I really must – This man is delicate, his brain has suffered much. He married Mina Murray …

Harker In the convent! They had to hold me upright, I was weak, so weak. Mina saved my life.

Seward The nuns told Mina she had turned up just in time. He was raving, babbling of dreadful things.

Woman What things?

Harker No! I could not tell you! They were … shaming.

Woman For heaven's sake, man, I'm a physician! There is nothing you could tell me, nothing in the world, that – *(More gently)* Is it what happened that led you to escape? To run away from Castle Dracula?

***Renfield** enters, with **Mina**. They approach **Harker** from behind. He does not see.*

Harker *(broken)* I was engaged. I had to be at home, I was to be married soon. And Dracula had warned me. That, I must admit.

Woman Warned you. But of what?

Harker About them. He showed me round my suite of rooms, and told me never, under any circumstance, to sleep outside of them.

Woman Why?

Harker The place was old, he said, with many … memories. Bad dreams for those who slept unwisely.

Woman Not very terrifying. As warnings go.

Harker Yes. I might have even laughed, I suppose. Except he made a washing motion with his hands, for if I disobeyed him. Like this. And the day before, of course – he'd tried to murder me.

Woman First murder, then bad dreams. I'll need convincing of the order. Go on, why the murder?

Harker I found a secret out. He walked up behind me as I shaved. I had a travel mirror in my hand, but he surprised me.

Renfield *(making **Harker** jump)* Like this, young sir? *(Laughs)* Lucky you didn't slit your little windpipe, eh, they're dangerous things them cut-throats, I use one.

Harker Renfield!

Renfield Not just for shaving, neither!

Harker *(to **Mina**)* And Mina. My beloved. Thank goodness you could come. *(To **Renfield**)* I used a safety, actually. A Swan.

Renfield New-fangled things, they won't catch on. Can't trust 'em nohow. If you wants a good clean cut.

Woman Mr Harker, you were telling me what happened. Or is it too 'shaming', now your wife is here?

Mina Don't mind me, I've heard it all before. I typed up his journals, didn't I?

Harker *(guiltily)* Dearest, it was you I loved. It was always you I loved.

Mina You're drivelling. Get on with it. The idea, that you could make me jealous. Ridiculous!

Harker You were not there! You do not know the half of it! There were three of them – so beautiful. They wanted me.

Woman But what about the secret you found out? Why did the count attack you?

Renfield Because his phizog* didn't show up in the mirror, did it? Mr Harker heard his voice, looked in the glass, and – nothing! Vampires don't have reflections, see? Upsets all round.

Harker *(comfortably)* Strangely enough, I found it more startling than upsetting, just at first. But then, I had seen so much in so short a time. The journey in itself, into the mountains, the peasants trying to detain me and forcing me to wear a crucifix around my neck, the fearful words I heard them muttering.

Seward *(from notes) Ordog* – Satan. *Pokol* – hell. *Stregoica* – witch. *Vrolok* – werewolf, or vampire.

Woman You are a linguist, Mr Harker?

Mina Hah! He translated some recipes for me, doctor. Absolute balderdash. Inedible.

Renfield More on his mind than paprika and impletata* dishes, mebbe! Foreign muck! Although, to be fair, there's no accounting for tastes now, is there?!

He opens his small box and pulls out a wriggling frog or mouse, which he pops into his mouth and chews noisily.

Seward Renfield. You'll be back in solitary if you don't behave.

Renfield Sorry Mr Seward, sir. Just bad habits dying hard.

Seward He thinks it'll give him eternal life, eating creepy-crawlies.

Renfield And you don't know the half of it, do you? Sorry, sir! Sorry!

Woman So you were startled, Mr Harker. You noticed this large, forbidding, aristocratic personage showing no reflection in your mirror, and you were merely startled. Can this be true?

Harker I was in a state of some confusion, as I've tried to indicate. More than a little startled, then, if that suits your expectations better. Whatever, enough to cut myself as my razor jumped. It was Dracula's reaction that was truly horrifying. His reaction to the blood.

---

* face

* stuffed aubergine

Renfield *(lip-smackingly)* Was it a bad cut, sir? Deep and penetrating?

Seward Renfield! I'm warning you!

Harker It was a safety razor, as I've said. Just a trickle down my chin.

Woman And? The Count's reaction?

Harker He tried to seize me. To get his talons in my throat. His eyes were blazing, he was demonic. I have no doubt he would have killed me.

Renfield *(excitedly)* Oh, he would've done. He would've bit your throat out, sir. There's nothing like a gush of fresh red throaty …

Seward Renfield! Leave the room! Go!

Renfield *(fawning)* Oh please, your worship! Forgive me just this once! I swear I'll …

Seward Go.

*He points imperiously, and **Renfield** goes, trailing his straitjacket.*

Mina *(languidly)* Jonathan, don't milk it too much, please. The tension's killing me.

Woman Did he attack you? Were you harmed?

Harker He touched the crucifix I had been given. He did not see it hidden at my throat. It made an instant change in him. The fury went. Evaporated.

Mina *(sarcastic)* Convenient.

Seward God's hand. In all of this God played a part. He watched over us.

Harker He said, 'Take care. Take care how you cut yourself. It is more dangerous than you think in this country.'

Seward Almost rational.

Harker Except that then he seized the shaving mirror from me and tore the heavy window open with one wrench of his terrible hand. He flung out the glass, which was shattered into a thousand pieces in the courtyard far below. It was very annoying.

Mina Annoying! Ye Gods and little fishes! *(Heavy irony)* And then you went and had some breakfast, I suppose!

Seward Mina, my dear. Your anger and frustration, though understandable ...

Mina The man is clearly mad! The marriage must be annulled, immediately!

Seward And you are clearly in denial, as we doctors call it.

Mina I deny that! Absolutely!

Harker I did go for breakfast. I freely admit it, what else could I do? I was a prisoner! A prisoner! I knew it then, and knew I could only dash myself onto the rocks a thousand feet below to get away! I went and had some breakfast, all alone. Count Dracula had disappeared, as he did so very often. In all that mighty castle ... I was alone.

Pause.

Woman Tell us about the 'shaming' parts, Mr Harker. The dreadful secrets you gabbled to the nuns. Where do they fit into it?

Mina Yes, come on, Jonathan. Let's hear it from the horse's mouth. I shall take some shorthand. Evidence for the divorce. In black and white.

Seward He is asleep. I think we have exhausted him.

Mina Convenient again. But we'll be back, my love. Sweet dreams!

*Lights fade. **Mina** leaves. **Attendants** stare ahead.*

Seward She loved him very much, you know. It was only seven years ago. It was a terrible ordeal. For all of us.

Woman Seven years ago. How time flies.

*They leave in darkness. **Harker** is left on the bed.*

Scene Two

Lights rise, red, not high. Enter **Dracula***. He wears a huge black cloak with a high, stiff collar that encases his head. He stands over* **Harker***.*

Dracula *(not directly to him)* I do not ask for much, my young friend. Some information only, some expertise. I am a *boyar**, and in my veins has flowed the blood of those who fought for lordship, as the lion fights. We fought the Huns, and joined Attila's blood with ours, we joined with the Ugric and the Berserkers, we mingled blood for blood with Lombards, Avars and the Bulgar hordes. We were claimed as kindred by the victorious Magyars, and crossed the Danube to beat the Turk and bring him shame and slavery. Ah sir, the Draculas can boast a record that the Hapsburgs and the Romanoffs can never reach. I do not ask for much. Only to expand, to spread, to find fresh fields and pastures new. Why do you thwart me?

Harker *(still on his back, unmoving)* Sir, I was sent to help you, but I do not know your wishes. What is it you require me to do?

Dracula Of all the Draculas there is but me alive. Blood is precious and there are only peasants left. Where ends the war without a brain and heart?

Harker I beg of you. I must return to England.

Dracula Write letters, then. You will stay another month.

Harker *(sitting up abruptly)* A month! That is too long! I am engaged!

Dracula I will take no refusal! It was agreed that you would help me!

Harker *(broken)* But I am a prisoner. You talk all night of ancient history, then leave me to my own devices every day. You give me food but do not eat, you tell me not to sleep out of my chamber, on pain of death or worse! For heaven's sake, sir, I am full of horrible imaginings! My nerves are growing quite destroyed!

---

* aristocrat

Dracula And I sympathize! Tomorrow you will construct some letters for me, good exercise for your active brain. One to Whitby, on the north-east coast, one to Carfax, which I plan to buy. It has a chapel all of its own, and a little crypt where an ancient soul like mine might find some rest! A central home as well I'll need, let's say in Paddington, London's heart. Fitting work for a solicitor, my friend. The time will race away!

Harker Race away? A month to write three letters? My poor dear Mina ...

Dracula You are a lucky man, having one who waits. When we get to England, Mr Harker – perhaps you will introduce me? I have an image in my mind. Long, slender neck. White and soft and yielding.

Harker Count Dracula!

Dracula *(laughing)* Forgive me, just an old man's fantasy. I cannot resist a neck! Away, I must to business. Explore, if you are bored. But remember what I said, if you are drowsy, do not forget. Farewell!

When he has gone, ***Harker*** *hurries to a window and cranes out. Then to another, then another. The lights are going dimmer.*

Harker After he had left me, not hearing any sound for quite some while, I quit my room and went up a stone stair to where I could look out across the south, a beautiful expanse bathed in yellow moonlight, whose very loveliness seemed bound to cheer me; there was peace and comfort in each breath I drew. But as I leaned out, my eye was caught by something moving below me, where the windows of the Count's own room would be. And what I saw was this.

The lights are almost gone.

Harker The Count's head, large and leonine*, was coming from the window. Slowly, like a tortoise's emerging from its shell. Then the whole man came out, on to the wall, just like a lizard,

---

* lion-like

or a cockroach. He hung there upside down, his cloak spread round him like some dreadful wings. I saw him move along and sideways at an awful speed, face downwards into that abyss, so very like a hateful lizard. And when he vanished into some other hole or window in the wall, I knew that I was lost, forsaken, that I would never see my home or my beloved Mina any more. I stumbled blindly through some rooms and doors, and went upstairs and down. I was tired and I found a bed at last, a couch I did not know. The Count's grim warning was clearly in my mind, but I took a certain pleasure in the act of disobeying. I felt sleepy, and I lay me down for sleep. And suddenly – I was not alone.

By now, ***Harker*** *is lying on his couch. On his last words – blackout.*

Scene Three

A beam of moonlight cuts the blackness. The two silent ***attendants*** *are transformed. They have dark, lustrous hair, red gowns, bare feet, bone-white faces. As they stare a third glides in, white gown and long fair hair. It could almost be* ***Mina****. They approach sensuously. The moonlight spreads.*

Vamp One I have a longing. He has such a pretty throat.

Fair girl And a deadly fear. See it in his smile.

Vamp Two I have a great desire. Wicked. Burning me. I have to kiss those red, red lips.

Fair girl He has a sweet fiancée. If she should know, this would be a stabbing pain for her.

Vamp One My teeth are sharp as razors. Oh Englishman, I would not hurt you, I would do no harm.

Vamp Two Mine are white, like pearls against my ruby lips, voluptuous. Oh Englishman, your bride is pale and lifeless, next to us.

Fair girl It would cause her pain. To think he wanted our sweet love, robust and sinuous*. But it would be the truth.

Vamp One The hardest pain of all. That he could want our easy love.

Fair girl To know we wanted *him*. That would be the hardest truth to bear. For if a woman wants a man, like that, in our wild and wanton* way – what hope has he of *mastery*?!

Vamp Two Ah, we *have* a master!

Vamp One But if this one falls to us – we have a slave!

Vamp Two *(to* ***fair girl****)* Go on! You first! Yours is the right to start!

Vamp One He's young and strong. There are kisses for us all.

---

* full of curves and turns; also devious

* unrestrained

The ***fair girl*** *kneels on the bed.* ***Harker*** *stretches languidly and invitingly, almost sighing with anticipation.*

VAMP ONE He can feel your breath. Sweet, oh honey-sweet.

VAMP TWO Oh anticipation! Oh delight! See how his eyelids quiver!

VAMP ONE See how his nostrils flare! He smells the blood upon your breath, your teeth!

The ***fair girl*** *licks her lips, half groaning. Eye-teeth bared.*

VAMP ONE My skin is tingling. Me next. Please, *me*.

VAMP TWO Oh languorous*. My heart is beating. Ecstasy.

The ***fair girl*** *takes* ***Harker's*** *neck into her mouth – and* ***Dracula*** *bursts in. Lights full. In one hand he has a sack, and with the other tears the* ***fair girl*** *away. The* ***women*** *drop back, hissing at him.*

DRACULA How dare you touch him! It is forbidden! This man belongs to me! To *me*!

FAIR GIRL *(contempt)* Hah! What good is he to you!? You do not love! You never love! What do you want with him?!

VAMP ONE We want to join with him.

VAMP TWO We need his blood.

FAIR GIRL You don't love any more. You never love.

DRACULA *(soft and penetrating)* Yes, I can love. Do you not remember it? And when I've done with him, I promise you, you shall have your turn. You shall kiss him at your will. Now go!

VAMP TWO But, Master ...

VAMP ONE Lord ...

DRACULA Away! I must waken him. There is much to do.

---

* dreamy relaxation

They hesitate. He raises a hand. The sack in his other hand begins to wriggle and twitch. Sulkily, they move away.

Fair girl Are we to have nothing, then? Tonight?

Dracula Ach, I am too soft with you. Too soft.

He tosses them the bag, from which comes the sudden sound of a baby crying. They mob onto it, shrieking joyfully, and carry it offstage. Lights fade to black on ***Dracula's*** *smile. The baby's wails fade.*

Scene Four

***Seward** at the table, **Morris** and **Lord Godalming** at the side. **Harker**, slumped and motionless, is on the couch. **Renfield** is opposite **Seward**, in a straitjacket.*

SEWARD Renfield, you are getting worse. I treat and treat and treat you – and you get worse. Ingratitude!

RENFIELD *(indicating **Harker**) I* get worse! What about him? A holiday in Transylvania and he comes back like that! Like a wet week in Southend! He might as well have kissed a ghost! He's barking.

HARKER *(bitterly)* Three ghosts. Oh please God, save me!

SEWARD Mr Harker is not ill, he's tired. His trip was long and arduous. He is not an inmate, either, he is a guest, a friend. It's you we're talking of. Can you explain yourself?

RENFIELD A fellow's got to eat, I do suppose.

SEWARD We weaned you off the spiders and the bugs. I begged, implored you to see the reason for that ban. And then you trapped the birds. Poor little sparrows flocking to your window.

RENFIELD Well *they* appreciates a good fat juicy bluebottle.

SEWARD And where are they now? How have you got rid of them?

RENFIELD I wouldn't have had to if you'd given me that cat.

SEWARD No cat! You are disgusting!

RENFIELD *(dreamy)* Just a kitten, really. A nice, sleek, playful little kitten. To teach, and play with, and to feed. To feed, that's my desire, Doctor Seward. To feed and feed.

SEWARD You have eaten them, Mr Renfield. You will admit it, sir! You have eaten those poor sparrows that you trapped!

RENFIELD They flew away. They polished off my bugs and flies, and scarpered.

SEWARD There were feathers in your room! Fresh blood spots on your pillow! Why do you deny it? You have eaten them!

Suddenly, ***Renfield*** *retches horribly. He cannot use his hands, so jack-knifes as he falls, coughing and vomiting.* ***Seward*** *jumps up.*

SEWARD Attendants! Nurse! Come quickly! Come!

Nothing happens. The coughing fit subsides.

SEWARD You know what this means, Renfield. You have gone a shade too far. It is time for Abraham Van Helsing. The heavy guns.

He stalks out. After a moment, ***Renfield*** *gets easily to his feet and sits as if nothing has happened. He smiles at* ***Godalming*** *and* ***Morris****.*

RENFIELD Van Helsing, eh? That should put the cat among the pigeons. Whoops! My sense of humour! But he's as famous in his way as Siggy Fraud of Old Vienna*. And as crazy. Do you eat cats and pigeons, by the way? I'm sorry, no one took the time to introduce us. The manners here is terrible, ain't they?

They look at each other nervously. They do not reply.

RENFIELD Hoity-toity, eh? Too grand to speak, is it? Next you'll be telling me you ain't mad, at all. So what you doing in the loony-bin?

MORRIS Ahem; we're visiting. We're friends of Doc Seward. And poor Jonathan there. I'm from America. Quincey Morris. Quincey P. Morris.

GODALMING Arthur Holmwood, Lord Godalming. Also a friend. And of Van Helsing, ditto, so don't be too impertinent, will you?

RENFIELD *Lord* Godalming? Not Lord Godalmighty? Are you really a lord, or are you gibbering?

---

* Sigmund Freud, Austrian psychiatrist (1856–1939)

Morris He's the *jenuwine ardickle*. He's got certificates.

Renfield Me, too. I was certified a dozen years ago. I met a man in Transylvania and – well, never mind. He's coming for me soon, he's on the boat to Merrie England. I'm on a promise.

Godalming A man from Transylvania. Who would that be?

Renfield Oh, just the Master. The keeper of my soul. He liberated me. He set me free of all travails.

Morris *Just* the Master! That's kinda neat. Democracy.

Harker *(suddenly)* Democracy, yes! Government by Demons! Yes!

Renfield *(comfortably)* Now, Mr Harker there is mad, whatever Dr Seward says. He was driven mad by hungry female women, the Master's little trollops got to him. I was bitten by the same bug, so to speak, but I fell to the Master, not his maids. They were much more dangerous.

Godalming That is ridiculous. Women are the weaker vessel, everyone knows that. You are spouting Socialism, sir!

Renfield Not I! I am spouting truth! I sold my soul to the Master, and I am waiting for his Second Coming.

Harker Blasphemy!

Renfield But the Master does not need me, which is my tragedy. I cannot spread his glory, I cannot pass it on. Would any of you let me drink your blood? Clamp my eager mouth around your yielding neck? You would not! I am not a woman! I do not have that power over you! The power of lust!

Furiously, ***Godalming*** *and* ***Morris*** *get to their feet.*

Godalming Good God, sir, this is monstrous! Seward! Attendants!

Renfield Women cannot help themselves! He overwhelms them! They are lost to normal men, they need men only to infect them in their turn, to do the Master's mighty work. They are enslaved, they in their turn enslave. It is His purity. It is the Master's sacred curse.

Godalming Seward! Have him confined!

***Seward** bursts in, with **attendants**. But **Renfield** is now calm.*

Renfield Don't strike me, Doctor. I am better now. You'll have to let me off this time, gents. Sorry, I got carried away.

Godalming Unconscionable! You disgrace the name of Englishman!

Morris I could get some men to work him over later, Seward. That is the Yankee way.

Renfield What, beat me to death? I'm invincible. Any case, the police would get involved.

Seward But people die in lunatic asylums, Mr Renfield. You know that. Suicide, for instance. It is a hazard of the game. Take him away. The padded cell, I think.

Renfield You promised me Abraham Van Helsing, and I get a padded cell instead. A lunatic can't trust anyone these days.

*He is bustled out by the **attendants**.*

Morris By Jiminy, that is one mad critter, Doc.

Godalming But where *is* Van Helsing?

Seward He follows on. He wanted Mrs Harker to be here. He wants to meet her, and her husband. Ah, Mina.

*She enters, followed by the **woman doctor**. **Harker** remains slumped.*

Godalming My dear. How good to see you.

Mina Lord Godalming. I'm charmed. And Quincey.

Morris The charming goes for me as well, dear Mrs H. With knobs on.

Seward Now. Let me present you to our most distinguished visitor. The most famous, the most eminent person in our field. Colleague, bring him in.

The ***woman*** *holds open the door, and a large man enters. He wears an enveloping dark cloak and a large floppy hat. He bows.*

SEWARD Wilhelmina – Professor Abraham Van Helsing, of Amsterdam. MD, PhD, Doctor of Literature, master to my servant, teacher in my humble quest for knowledge. In this current matter he can help us as no other man alive could do. His skill, his knowledge, his experience, are quite unparalleled.

Mina *moves forward to shake* ***Van Helsing's*** *hand, but he kisses hers.*

MINA Oh. Professor.

VAN HELSING Madame. So deeply, deeply charming.

GODALMING By Jove. Not the British way!

MORRIS *(to* ***Mina****)* You've heard of him, I guess? He did a lecture tour back Stateside*.

MINA Of course. *(Sharply)* Jonathan! Surely you could stand, at least? This man has come a long long way to help you!

Harker *gets reluctantly to his feet, and turns to face* ***Van Helsing*** *– who throws his cloak wide open, throws back his head, and sweeps off his hat.* ***Harker*** *is transfixed with horror, and collapses to his knees.*

HARKER Oh heavens be my aid and comforter! Oh Lord God, it is he! It is the Prince of Evil!

He sprawls on his face. ***Van Helsing*** *stands above him, arms spread out.*

VAN HELSING *(maybe speaking with a strong accent)* Van Helsing, not ze Prince of Evil, oh dear no! This man seems much deluded, my dear friends. So I will help him. I can see, you know, into the human soul ...

MINA Jonathan, for pity's sake get up! You are my husband! Oh, this is embarrassing.

---

* in the United States

***Van Helsing**, his cloak dropping all around them vampire-like, bends to **Harker's** neck, listening, perhaps, to his breathing.*

VAN HELSING *(lifting his head)* Yes, very strong is the delusion. *(He stands)* Good people, you had better leave me now. I wish to confer with Mr Harker and dear, good Madam Mina, his so lovely wife. I must achieve a diagnosis. The delusion is distressingly severe.

MORRIS We'll leave you to it happily, Professor. Poor Jonathan. He is in need of something, clearly. I'm damned if we could give it to him, though.

GODALMING The things he suffered in that dreadful land. Please God that you can make him well again.

SEWARD Lord Godalming, Mr Morris – tea in my quarters I believe would hit the spot? Come, Doctor.

*They all leave. **Harker** remains on the floor, but taking notice.*

VAN HELSING Now, Madam Mina. Dr Seward has communicated some of the details by telegraph machine to Amsterdam. You fill the gaps, flesh out the portrait, as it were. Would you care to lie upon the couch?

***Harker** jumps up and leaps on it, frenziedly.*

HARKER *My* couch! *Mine!* How dare you, Doctor! I thought you understood!

VAN HELSING You thought I was the Prince of Darkness, also. Now calm yourself. Be calm.

MINA *(quietly)* I am not the mad one, Doctor. I think my point is made.

VAN HELSING Then tell me everything. You have been married long?

MINA Long? No, six weeks or less. It seems like longer, though.

VAN HELSING You have troubles, I can see. In such short time. So when did it go wrong?

Mina When he went away to Transylvania. We were engaged. He did not write.

Harker I did write! But Dracula ... There was no postal service!

Van Helsing Were you in love?

Mina Of course we were.

Harker Whatever love means.

Mina I knew. We were very ordinary, Professor, but I knew what love was. And he left our dreary world, our dim, dull, boring world – to be seduced.

Harker No! I was not unfaithful to you! Not guilty, Mina! It was my blood they wanted! My manhood! My humanity!

Mina Three women came in the dead of night, and joined him in his bed. And he says that he was not unfaithful! Hah!

Harker No! I was seeking something else. Something more important!

Van Helsing A good line for an adulterer, admittedly. What *were* you seeking, do you believe?

Harker Life! Fulfilment! I don't know! They were amazing creatures! They were wonderful!

Van Helsing And your little pale fiancée, meek and mouselike – forgive me, Madame Mina – so dull, so ordinary, sitting back at home. One can see that you were tempted. How bitter the fight must have been.

Mina *(sarcastic)* Oh yes, he really fought! And he'd been alone the whole time he was in Transylvania, that's what he told me first! There was nobody, he said, except his host. The liar.

Harker There was no one! No servants, footmen, cooks or grooms. There was nobody!

Van Helsing How did you get there, then? Up the Borgo Pass on foot?

Harker Well, there was a coachman. But I have reason to believe he was the Count, as well.

Van Helsing I beg your pardon? *(He stands, swinging back his cloak and shoulders: **Dracula** to the life)* How could this be? How could one man be another?

Mina He is a liar, that is how. A liar and a lunatic.

Harker No! Not a liar! Neither of those things! Oh, you behave so innocently, but where were you while I was suffering? You talk of fallen virtue, where were you? I'll tell you, Doctor! She was with a pro ... with a person whose ... whose downward path was ... Who was making free with several men! At once!

Mina *(stands, stamping with rage)* How dare you, Jonathan! Lucy Westenra is dead! How dare you speak so ill of her! Professor, this man is ... he is my husband, so I must forgive him, I try to understand. But he was mad in Transylvania, he was infected with this disease he brought back home. I rescued him in Budapest, and married him, but he boasts of women in his bed, 'amazing' women, 'wonderful' – and yet insults my spotless virtue, and my friend's. I cannot stand it, Doctor. It can not go on!

She sweeps out. Silence.

Harker *(calmly)* She is obsessed, you see. If I did find temptation in that gloomy castle I got over it, I survived by force of character, but Mina is a woman, she is weak; and therefore she's afraid that she will fall. She came to Budapest to find me because of things she saw and did in Whitby, with her friend. Lucy Westenra, poor little rich girl, the debutante* with everything my bride-to-be had not. *You* don't think my sin was lust, do you, Professor? *You* don't believe the fears and horrors of that awful land were fantasies? You do believe in Dracula, don't you? The vampire, the monster, *nosferatu**? Tell me you believe and I'm not mad.

***Van Helsing** crouches over him, enveloping him. They embrace.*

Harker *(brokenly)* I saw him in his coffin. After the seduction night. I went into the dungeons and found the women's tombs. And the living body of their Lord, resting on unholy earth. You do believe me, don't you?

---

* a young upper-class woman, formally presented to society

* the undead

Now ***Van Helsing*** *lifts his head.*

VAN HELSING Oh I believe, friend Jonathan. I believe. Who knows what really happened to Lucy Westenra on holiday in Whitby, I did not meet her – or your own dear Madam Mina – until afterwards. But in Dracula the monster I believe. Oh yes, indeed I do.

As the lights fade, is that blood, leaking from his mouth?

Scene Five

The couch is now a gravestone. Sitting on it, head in hands, is **Lucy Westenra**, *pretty, young, and reminiscent of the* **woman doctor**. *She is crying.* **Mina** *sits beside her comforting her.*

81

MINA But Lucy, darling, I can't see what you're crying for. We're on holiday, the weather's wonderful – and three men proposed to you in a single day last week! Good golly – one of them's of noble birth! Lord Godalming! As rich as Croesus*!

LUCY Mina, money isn't everything. Sometimes I wish it was, it would make choosing so much easier. Don't you see, don't you understand? I feel so wanton.

MINA It's not your fault though, is it? How can you help it if three men want you desperately? I'm engaged as well. I long to marry when my Jonathan returns from Transylvania. Does that make me wanton, too?

LUCY One of mine would have been so wonderful for you, my suitor Number Two. If you had not had Jonathan, of course! He's handsome, by no means poor, good English yeoman stock – and runs his own immense lunatic asylum at only nine and twenty. Oh, the choice was terrible!

MINA Jonathan expects great things, however. Mr Hawkins thinks very highly of him. He'd have to, wouldn't he? To send him all that way to do negotiations with a count?

LUCY Oh, of course Jonathan's wonderful. He's very suitable for you, so kind and ... steady. And money's not a problem is it, all the time you can keep your little bits of work?

MINA We'll muddle through. And who is Number Three? Is he well-off, as well?

LUCY He's American! He's rolling in it, if you'll excuse my slang. He talks it all the time – although not in front of servants, naturally; he has exquisite manners for a foreigner – and I find him very funny and adventurous. Oh, the tales he tells, so wild, such

---

* the last king of Lydia (circa 560–546 BC), noted for his wealth

derring-do! I suppose that we women are such cowards that we think a man will save us from fears, and we marry them.

Mina Well, I'm not sure about Jonathan saving me from anything – although he does write excellent shorthand; he's very clever. And I'm sure he's faithful to me, too.

Lucy Of course he is! Oh Mina, why are men so noble when we women are so little worthy of them? I even kissed poor Quincey – that's his name, Quincey P. Morris: he's from Texas – although I knew that he was not the final one for me.

Mina Not the final one? Well, a chaste kiss is perhaps...

Lucy Chaste? Yes. There'd been a perfect torrent of love-making, Mina; he'd lain his very heart and soul out. What else could I do? And then Arthur – Lord Godalming – came in later and in seconds I was in his arms, and kissing him as well.

Mina Oh dear, Lucy. You are very bold.

Lucy Don't look at me like that! Don't disapprove! Oh Mina, why can't they let a girl marry three men, or as many as want her, and save all this trouble?

Mina Lucy!

Lucy Yes, it is heresy, I know! I must not say it! But I'll be twenty in six months, and I want to live. I want to taste experience, I need excitement. I want to marry, and … and …

Mina *(carefully)* Do you mean … offspring?

Lucy Now who's being bold?! But … yes, I suppose I do. Oh no I don't! Oh Mina, we've been … we've told all our secrets to each other since we were *children*. Can't you guess? Oh, you'll think me such a horrid … flirt.

Mina Not babies, then? But how a flirt? Lucy, I just don't understand.

Lucy I've chosen, Mina. I really think I have. It's Arthur Holmwood, Lord Godalming. Oh, the kisses were so wonderful. I know. I'm sure I know.

Mina You *think* you've chosen? You're *sure* you know? Lucy, forgive me, but ...

Lucy That's it! A flirt! You think I'm just a flirt! Mina, it's so very *hard* to choose.

Mina But it is Lord Godalming? You told him you'd accept? You are engaged?

Lucy We are, we are, we are! I will never let him down, never, in thought or word or deed. *(Pause)* But ...

Mina But what? Lucy, but *what*?

Lucy When Dr Seward – my Number Two, the lunatic asylum man – well, when *he* asked me if I would be his wife, he kept playing with his scalpel. I found it ... my imagination ... I couldn't keep my eyes off it. It almost made me ... scream.

Mina Horrible. That was horrible for you.

Lucy But it wasn't! Well, not exactly horrible. Mina – you'll be married soon, like me. Both of us. It was not exactly horrible, and nor was kissing Quincey. There's a ... it's a sort of yearning in the soul. Don't you feel it too? At all?

Mina I don't know what you mean, my dear. I'm sure I do not have the ghost of an idea.

Lucy Well men, they say – I must be devastatingly frank, dear Mina – they say men – oh, why are they so *superior*, it isn't *fair*. If they had doubts, if they found making choices as hard as women do ...

Mina *Some* women, Lucy; have a care!

Lucy I'm sorry dear, some women. Yes, I didn't mean that you – I'm sorry, Mina, try to forgive me.

She covers her face. ***Mina*** *embraces her.*

Mina Dear little thing, dear friend. I think you're worrying unduly. The choice might seem hard but now you've come away to Whitby surely all will turn out perfectly, that's what holidays are for. The sea air is such a bracer, too. And you have decided, haven't you? You're set on it? Lord Godalming. It is such a noble name.

Lucy Arthur. Arthur Holmwood. But yes, I'll be a lady.

Mina God willed it so. You could have had no other.

Lucy You are so wise, dear Mina. It is just – we women are so weak.

Mina Lucy Westenra! Not even as a joke! My Jonathan is far away across that rolling ocean but I trust in him as he in me. I know he will be safe. We are not weak. We're strong.

The sky is darkening. Perhaps a roll of thunder. ***Lucy*** *is gloomy.*

Lucy Look at the storm clouds gathering out there, though. I feel that something – gigantic – is going to happen very soon.

Mina Yes, dear. Marriage, and all that state entails. I long for it. Do not you?

Lucy I long for something. Something... extraordinary.

Mina Three men did battle for your hand! Three men between them handsome, rich, exotic! What more extraordinary than that? I don't know what you have to fear!

Lucy Perhaps the lack of fear itself. Perhaps I need some wildness, terror, glory! Oh, if once I felt it, Mina, I would be *truly* lost. Truly, truly, deeply – and for ever! Oh, I long for it.

It is almost dark.

Mina *(stiffly)* I think it is a good thing you are to marry soon, Lucy. You need a man to exercise restraint on you. Strong we women may be, but we must above all things be respectable. I thank the Lord He gave me Jonathan.

Silence.

Lucy Look at the sea now, Mina. So wild, and beautiful, and bleak. *That* is exciting, Mina, so exciting. It is so full of *life*.

Scene Six

***Seward** at the table, facing **Renfield**, who is still straitjacketed. Near to them are **Morris** and **Godalming**. The silent **attendants** in their places.*

SEWARD So he came ashore in a hurricane, did he? This is nonsense, Renfield. We do not have them in this country. *Quod erat demonstrandum.*

MORRIS He's tall and thin and handsome, you keep telling us, but no one saw him land. He's invisible as well, is he?!

GODALMING There is a police force even in the north of England, I believe. And coastguards, too.

RENFIELD The ship was wrecked. Grounded in a storm. Blown up on the beach.

SEWARD It's summer, man! This is too absurd, even for a God-forsaken hole like Whitby. It's August!

RENFIELD Unnatural, granted. Worst storm in living memory, all the journals was agreed. And in the midst of it a foreign ship, Black Sea rigged, with one man at the steering wheel and him stone dead. My master, Lord Dracula.

SEWARD Make your mind up, man. If it was your master, how could he have been stone dead?

RENFIELD It wasn't him tied to the steering wheel you fools, that was the skipper. *He* was dead!

GODALMING So a dead man sailed the vessel into Whitby? Through that narrow entrance, past those reefs? Excellent seamanship. For a corpse.

RENFIELD The Master was lying in his coffin in the hold. As he had been all the way from Varna. If the man had been alive, how come he piled her on the beach once she was through the entrance?

MORRIS If your so-called master got her through the entrance – or got a dead man to! – why hit the shore at all? He could have drowned getting through the breakers.

Renfield Little you know then, Americano. Dogs can swim. And they can't get themselves arrested!

Godalming Dogs? Oh, God save us all.

Renfield Too late for that, friend. The Master's come, his work is to the purpose. His cargo on the ship was coffin-loads of earth, sacred or profane* depending on your point of view. Just because he turned to dog to beat the waves and rescuers don't mean he can't turn back again. He can be anything, anything he likes, a mist, a wolf, a great big flapping bat. First he'll get your women, I expect. Then they'll suck your lives away together.

Seward Attendants! We have borne enough! Get him away again! Renfield, this time is final, you will not emerge! You're in your cell for good.

Morris Damn good riddance too, I say.

Godalming Seward, you are far too lenient.

As the ***attendants*** *approach,* ***Renfield*** *rushes them. He is soon dragged down, but kicks and struggles for a while. He makes a sort of speech.*

Renfield *(roaring)* I am here to do your bidding, master. I am your slave, and you will reward me, I have worshipped long. Now you are near, I await your commands, and you will not pass me by, will you, dear master, in your distribution of good things?

Godalming Disgusting, disgusting! Let him be gone!

Seward The padded cell! Immediately!

Renfield *(as he goes, resigned)* I shall be patient, master. It is coming – coming – coming.

Morris You ought to throw away the blessed key!

---

* ungodly; blasphemous

Scene Seven

Lucy *lying on the bed, with* ***Dracula*** *bending over her, shrouded in his cloak. It is night, very dim. He appears to be biting her neck. As lights rise, we see* ***Seward*** *at his table, facing* ***Mina.*** *Two* ***attendants*** *in their places.*

Mina She had not been sleeping, I remember. Ever since the dreadful storm. In fact she was sometimes half-asleep, sometimes sleepwalking.

Seward You shared a bedroom all the time in Whitby?

Mina We were on holiday. It was a tiny house. On the night of the storm she got out of bed and dressed herself. Twice.

Seward All the time asleep?

Mina I managed to undress her and put her back between the sheets both times without her waking up. Next day we heard a dog had killed another dog, torn its throat out in the town. A massive dog. It was all material for her dreadful dreams.

Seward Was your sleep at all disturbed?

Mina I slept very lightly. Jonathan was in Transylvania, I had not had word of him for ages, I worried. Three nights after the ship had come ashore I woke up broad awake and sat up with an awful sense of fear on me. It was nearly one a.m. and Lucy's bed was empty. I lit a match and she was not in the room.

Seward Were you terrified?

Mina Her dressing gown and clothes were there, so I was reassured. But the hall door was ajar; it is always locked at night. I put on a heavy shawl and ran.

Seward Where were you going?

Mina Up to the headland. Our favourite sitting place by the ruined abbey. As I climbed up I saw her suddenly, as a black cloud rolled away from the moon. She was snowy white, in her nightdress, half reclining. I was still some way away.

Seward Half reclining?

Mina On our favourite seat. Among the gravestones. Her head was stretched out backwards, across the rail, her neck was white and ... open. And behind her ...

Seward Yes?

Mina I could not be sure. Maybe my memory...

Seward You saw something else, though? You think.

Mina Somebody else. Oh, I don't know! Man or beast, I could not tell! I flew along the fish market, I trailed up endless steps, but my feet seemed like lead weights. There was something, undoubtedly. Something long and black, bending over her poor white figure.

Seward Did you not call?

Mina I shouted. I shouted out in fright: Lucy! Lucy! And something raised a head – from where I was I could just see a face. White face. Red, gleaming eyes. Then darkness, then the moon again, it struck so brilliantly. Lucy was quite alone, no living thing, at all, apart from her. Not a sign.

Seward What did she say? When you got close to her?

Mina She was asleep. Her lips were parted and she was breathing, long heavy gasps, as though she had to struggle to get her lungs full. I was afraid to wake her suddenly, but in pinning my shawl round her, to keep her warm, I thought I must have pricked her. There were two marks. On her neck. She bled a little.

Seward She woke up then, of course?

Mina No, not then. I woke her very gently when I'd wrapped her up. She was confused and sleepy but I got her home to bed. She slept until midday.

Seward And the pinpricks?

Mina Let's not be ridiculous, Dr Seward. They never healed. Some weeks later, Lucy Westenra was dead. Back home in the south of England, at Hillingham.

Seward You were abroad by then?

Mina I felt I had abandoned her. I had to go to Budapest to save Jonathan. I had been summoned by the nuns. He was in a convent hospital; he'd had a mental breakdown. I saved Jonathan and damned my friend. Poor Lucy died without me.

Seward But she was not alone.

Pause.

Mina They tell me she was not alone.

Mina Harker *gets up, and slowly leaves.*

Scene Eight

*When **Mina** has gone, **Seward** stands and walks slowly to the bed. **Morris** and **Godalming** come in and also converge. As they arrive, the bent figure straightens, shifts his cloak, reveals himself. It is **Van Helsing**.*

SEWARD Van Helsing. It was good of you to come. Arthur, he knows as much about obscure diseases as anybody in the world. If anyone can save dear Lucy, it is he.

GODALMING Please God, sir, that you can. We are due to marry very soon.

VAN HELSING Sir, Dr Seward here saved my own life once, which is why I have come hot-foot, as I believe you English say. Miss Westenra, I must confess, is very, very ill.

MORRIS She is worse than yesterday, Professor.

VAN HELSING Worse? How so?

MORRIS I was shocked when I saw her then; today I'm horrified. The red's gone from her gums, even. She's paler than a ghost.

VAN HELSING I'm afraid that I agree. She is suffering from want of blood. The heart's action is not what it should be.

SEWARD Want of blood? But we gave her a transfusion when she came back home from Whitby yesterday! That was my diagnosis, as well!

GODALMING I drained my veins for her! I will again! I would give my last drop to save her!

VAN HELSING Young sir, I do not ask so much as that. Not the last. Go now. Go and rest. I will think.

GODALMING But if you knew how gladly I would die for her, you'd understand!

VAN HELSING I do, young friend, I do. You may take a little kiss from her, then go. Take Mr Quincey Morris too, to comfort you. John Seward here and me are doctors. We better understand.

Morris Heck, Art – that's the best advice. Leave it to the medics, I say. Come.

Godalming *(gravely)* I will kiss her. I will kiss her as my bride. The transfusion of my blood into her veins has made her truly mine. In God's eyes, we are married.

*He kisses **Lucy**, and they leave. The **attendants** go, too. **Van Helsing** gets a tube and scalpel from his bag and prepares them.*

Van Helsing No time to lose. Is it you or me?

Seward I am younger and stronger, Professor. It must be me.

Van Helsing Roll up your sleeve. You must bear the pain without an opiate, I fear. We will do it blood to blood, your vein to hers.

*They stand next to **Lucy**. **Van Helsing** cuts her vein, inserts the tube, and connects it to **Seward's** arm.*

Seward My blood might waken her. Invigoration.

Van Helsing I shall take precautions. *(He prepares a syringe)* A hypodermic injection of morphia. There. That is better. Need I say, John, breathe no word of this to Godalming.

Seward Naturally. He is her fiancé.

Van Helsing You love her too though, *niet waar*? I can see the signs, my friend. You are a man; it is a man we want. To see it would make Godalming very jealous. It would frighten him.

Seward Oh Professor, you understand so much. No man could know, without experiencing the sensation, what it is to feel his own life drawn from his body into the woman that he loves.

Van Helsing If this should not go well, if she should need some more life essence, you may not be the last one, dear friend. A brave man is the best thing on this earth when a woman is in trouble.

Seward God sends men when they are needed.

Van Helsing Brave John. One, two, three all open up their veins for her. Beside ... perhaps ... even this old man. If she needs the blood of four strong men, then she shall have it. And this sweet maid becomes a polyandrist* in the eyes of Godalming – and me a bigamist* to Mother Church, which says that my dear wife still lives, although she's dead to me. Oh it is grim, the awful irony!

He laughs.

Seward *(stiffly)* It is, at least, no laughing matter. It is a case for desperate pity.

Van Helsing *(soberly)* And if you could look into my very heart, maybe you would pity me the most of all. Because I know.

Seward Know? Know what, though?

Van Helsing Do you mean to tell me, friend John, that you have no suspicion? Those marks upon her neck? All these strange and horrible events? Her state of health?

Seward Nervous prostration, surely? Following on great loss or waste of blood?

Van Helsing And how the waste, John? How the loss? You are a clever man – where has it gone? Why is there no sign to show for it? What took it out?

Seward Tell me! I can hazard no opinion! I do not have the data!

*He is leaning over **Lucy**, and with appalling suddenness, she bursts up from the couch and flings her arms about his neck, dragging him down upon her and sinking her face into his neck.*

Lucy Oh my love, my love! Kiss me, I am so glad that you have come! Kiss me!

***Van Helsing** springs on **Seward** and drags him off her by the neck, almost throwing him across the room.*

---

* a woman who is married to more than one man at the same time

* a person who marries when still legally married to someone else

Van Helsing Not for your life! Not for your living soul and hers!

The tube is plucked from **Lucy's** *arm. She gives an enraged cry, her teeth champing, and tries to suck on it.* **Van Helsing** *pulls it away. She jumps up, he raises a hand to her, and she runs offstage.*

Seward *(shaken)* She called me love. She called me love and tried to kiss me. But oh, her teeth are sharp. They're long.

Van Helsing John, your blood is in her now. It may not be too late to save her.

Seward But what is wrong?

Van Helsing We must use garlic. Crucifixes. We must seal up the doors and windows.

Seward *(almost laughs)* Garlic? Her illness then will be plain halitosis*!

Van Helsing I do not jest! There is grim purpose in all I do! Seal up the windows and Lucy Westenra will live. If the garlic is disturbed, who knows how baneful the result?

Seward We had better tell the servants. And her mother. She is unwell herself, poor thing.

Van Helsing Not her mother. She would not understand. The shock might kill her.

Seward Understand what though, Professor? I do not understand, myself.

Van Helsing And you my ablest student, of them all. It is hard, young Seward. It is hardest to believe. But if we cannot save dear Lucy Westenra, she will die and never die. The only way to save her then, and she undead, *nosferatu*, will be more terrible than we have done so far, far worse than strewing garlic at her door and window. What we must do will be … unspeakable.

Pause.

---

* bad breath

Seward The madman, Renfield, talked of 'the Master' coming. In the storm. In coffins of dank earth. He said his master can do... anything. But Renfield ... he is mad.

Van Helsing But who is sane, my friend? Just who is sane? I sometimes think we must all be mad and that we shall wake to sanity in strait-waistcoats.

Exit ***Van Helsing***.

Scene Nine

***Lucy** enters, pale and wan, led by the **attendants**. They lay her on the bed and place a necklet of garlic flowers round her, then strew others on the bed and at the windows, with **Seward** helping. **Lucy** sleeps, and the others leave her all alone. Very dim lights. Silence.*

*Then, **Lucy's mother** enters with a lamp. Long white nightgown, like a wedding dress. Hair grey and straggling. She walks to **Lucy**, looks at her.*

MOTHER Oh my dove, my darling little girl. What have they done to you? What is this ghastly stench? Ugh! Garlic! The weed the French use to destroy good food! It's choking you! It's *choking*!

*She tears the flowers from **Lucy's** neck and bundles them in her shawl, clears off the bed, then goes to the windows.*

MOTHER More of it! Oh, that ghastly Dutchman and his strange ideas! To leave the good fresh air of Whitby and come to this! It is so very smelly! It is like a charnel house*! And all the windows closed! Tight and locked and shuttered! Oh these foolish foreigners! *(Tears back shutters, opens windows)* There! Come in God's fresh air! Come in goodness! Oh, Dr Helsing, how you will thank me in the morning!

*She goes, and there is silence. Perhaps, shortly, the sound of heavy flapping, giant wings. And in the window, a huge black shape appears. **Dracula** moves to the bed, enveloping **Lucy** entirely in his cloak. He remains like that for some long silent seconds. Then – the lights flash up to full. The figure over **Lucy** leaps upright with a positive roar of rage. It is **Van Helsing**, beside himself with fury.*

VAN HELSING Old woman! What have you done! Oh God, God, God! Jack Seward! To me, quickly! Help!

***Seward** rushes in.*

SEWARD What is it? What's going on?

---

* a building where corpses or bones are left

Van Helsing This poor old mother! All unknowing! She does such thing as lose her daughter's body, and her soul! You must operate on me, instantly. Today the blood is mine! Where are the instruments?

Seward The tubes and scalpel in the other room! Brandy and opiates!

Van Helsing Help me! We'll take her with us! There is a fire there! Hot water! We do not have much time!

*They gather **Lucy** up and hurry out with her. Lights down.*

Scene Ten

Harker** is seated by the table, the two **attendants** at the side as usual. In front of **Harker** are **Morris** and **Godalming.

Morris *(in answer to **Harker**)* No, she did not die then, Jonathan. That time we saved her life. The Professor stripped off his shirt and pumped his blood into her, willy-nilly. What a good ol' boy.

Godalming He was the fourth one. I gave my blood, but it was not enough. I loved her so I gave my blood to her. I loved her so I let other men give theirs. Harker. That was so very, very hard.

Morris But she still died. The vampire outwitted us. Circumstances, bad luck, cunning from beyond the pit of hell.

Godalming A telegram from Antwerp went astray, so Seward did not know he had to guard her in Van Helsing's stead at Hillingham. Lucy let her mother sleep with her, and yet again the poor old lady displaced the garlic from her neck. God forgive her.

Morris The servant girls stole sherry, as the lower orders do, and Dracula had doctored it with laudanum. Next morning Jack Seward and Van Helsing got to the house together, and found the maids all crashed unconscious, drugged to the eyeballs. Lucy was dying, and her poor old mother lay in bed beside her, dead. The look of terror on her face was horrible.

Godalming *(brokenly)* Then Lucy took three more, long days, of unadulterated agony. I was at her bedside when she slipped away. She was like a tired child.

*He covers his face. **Morris** gently leads him to the bed. **Harker** alone.*

Morris He sobbed, Jonathan. He sobbed as I never knew men could. It nearly broke me, just to hear him sob.

***Van Helsing** and **Seward** enter, **Van Helsing** carrying a hammer and a stake. He stops, but **Seward** walks past the bed to his chair. Lights to front.*

Seward *(to **Harker**)* So that was how you heard the news? It was a *trauma*. Like an awful dream.

Harker An awful dream, or madness? They filled Miss Westenra with four men's blood, they poured their essence into her hungry body almost daily. But by night she weakened, until she could support no more. Was this sanity?

Seward Not sanity nor madness. It was necessity. There was no alternative.

Harker And afterwards? They cut her head off and destroyed her heart: they buried her in Highgate Cemetery, then dug her up, beheaded her, and hammered a great spike into her chest. Doctor, I swear to you, it's true! You're helping me in this, you are my only hope. I thought Van Helsing ... I thought then that he had done it all. I thought that he must be the evil genius. That it was all his fantasy, grotesque.

***Harker** stands. He is agitated.*

Seward *(calmly, after a pause)* But what about your time in Transylvania? The bloody handmaidens, the lizard-man who scuttled down the walls? Were they not real? Did you imagine them?

Harker *(pause)* No, I believed it. I admit it, I believed it all. But I wonder if my mind ... Van Helsing's mind ... I wonder if we all became unhinged?

Seward I am not unhinged. I run a mental hospital.

Harker But is it possible, do you think? That the Professor can have done it all himself? He is so abnormally clever that if he went off his head ...

Seward No, I shall not believe it. He is like Sigmund Freud, too great a marvel for mere mortal men like us to doubt or question. You must control yourself, or you will end up like Renfield. Van Helsing's mind is wonderful.

*Angry and impatient, **Seward** stands and joins the others near the bed.*

Harker *(struggling with himself)* But he said that Lucy was undead. Sweet Lucy Westenra. *(He moves towards the* ***attendants****, imploringly)* He said she left her tomb at night and bit the necks of little children that she snatched, and sucked their precious blood. He took us with him there one night, to Highgate, and made us wait for her return, to prove that it was real. He took poor Godalming and told him he must kill her. The man who'd sworn to be her husband! You must help me, you must help. It was a scene of unparalleled insanity. Unparalleled.

As the ***attendants*** *stand, the lights go down. At the back,* ***Van Helsing*** *is in silhouette, arms wide, the hammer and stake held out. In a moment,* ***Lucy*** *walks in, dreamily. Her hair is long, her face bone-white, crimson stains on mouth and breast.*

Godalming *(agonised)* Lucy! Oh God, my Lucy!

She stands and smiles at him. She is languorous, inviting.

Lucy Come to me, Arthur. Leave these others, come to me.

Godalming My darling.

He moves towards her, mesmerised.

Lucy My arms are hungry for you. Come, and we can rest together. Come, husband, come!

As he enters the embrace, ***Van Helsing*** *leaps forward with a roar, forming a crucifix with the stake and hammer.* ***Lucy*** *screams, as the others, including* ***Harker*** *and* ***attendants****, surge in and obscure her from the audience and bear her down onto the tomb, covering her body with a sheet.* ***Godalming*** *then spins to face the audience, the hammer and stake now in his hands.*

Godalming Van Helsing! Van Helsing! Tell me now what I must do!

Van Helsing The point into her heart! Press! Press! Your blessed hand shall strike the blow that sets her free. It is the hand that loved her best; the hand she would have chosen if God had let her choose. In His name strike! Strike with all your soul's humanity! Drive in that sacred point!

__Godalming__ turns and pushes through the ruck, with a despairing cry. The hammer hovers then comes crashing down. There is an awful scream; perhaps everyone joining in, a general cry of horror and regret. __Harker__ pushes out and speaks straight to the audience, as the hammer blows continue.

Harker *(flatly)* The Thing in the coffin writhed. A hideous screech came from the opened lips. The body shook and twisted in its wild contortions. The mouth was smeared with crimson foam. But Arthur never faltered as he drove in the mercy-bearing stake. Whilst the blood from the pierced heart welled and spurted round it. And then our voices rang in triumph through the narrow little vault.

Seward Hip-hip!

The rest Huzzah!

Seward Hip-hip!

The rest Huzzah!

Seward Hip-hip!

The rest Huzzah, huzzah, huzzah!

Silence. __Godalming__ walks wearily into view, the hammer in his hand, and falls onto his knees. __Van Helsing__, holding a bloody knife, comes and stands behind him.

Van Helsing I have cut her head off and filled her mouth with garlic. Now Arthur, my friend – am I not forgiven?

Pause.

Godalming God bless you that you have given her back her soul again. And me some peace.

Scene Eleven

***Mina** seated in front of the desk. **Attendants** as before. The **woman doctor** enters and sits facing **Mina**. She has a sheaf of notes.*

Woman Forgive my lateness, Mrs Harker. An unforeseen delay. Things do not always run smoothly even in …

Mina … the best run madhouses. I understand.

Woman *(checking notes)* So. Wilhelmina Harker, née Murray. Now … twenty-five, is it?

Mina Nearly twenty-six. I was still eighteen when all this happened. Still … happy.

Woman Strange thing to say.

Mina Why? Like Lucy I was on the verge of marriage. Unlike her I had not yet been awakened. My … womanhood was dormant. Completely. Hence my statement.

Woman So when the men … awakened her … it was her Fall, you think? But she had three, all vying for her favours. Which one did the wakening?

Mina None of those three milksops! You might as well ask me if Jonathan … well, never mind.

Woman You mean … Count Dracula?

Mina Your coyness is a little unconvincing, doctor. Who else but Dracula? He was everything that Lucy ever longed for. She threw herself into his arms, and showed them up for what they really were. She had to die. They could not have borne it if she'd lived. The knowledge killed her. Life.

Woman Life killed her? You're not making any sense. Have you had your medicine today?

Mina They knew, even if you pretend you don't. When Lucy died, they cut me off from it, they banned me from any further part in their investigation. Van Helsing was the worst. He told them that I had a man's brain – his idea of a compliment I believe – and a woman's heart. By which he meant that if Dracula should ever get his hands on me, I would be lost, like Lucy Westenra. I was a woman. And therefore I would fall. A martyr to temptation.

Woman But Mr Harker fell. In Transylvania.

Mina He did not fall, he tore himself away. Three lovely women went for him, and he survived by strength of personality. Lucy did not; she was a woman. She would have had all three milksops had it been allowed: she told me so herself, remember? But then she met Count Dracula – and she was lost.

Woman You make her sound very … weak.

Mina Not my opinion, this is *theirs*. She was a woman, that is what they fear. Dracula, unlike her other suitors, was irresistible. The first time he came to her, on the cliffs at Whitby, in the graveyard, he was a dog. He was an animal.

Woman *(note of triumph)* You said you could not tell. *(Consults notes)* 'Man or beast, I could not tell. Something long and black, red gleaming eyes, white face'. Dogs don't have white faces, Mrs Harker, do they?

Mina But dogs are wild and elemental and they bite. Maybe it was neither man nor beast. Have you considered that?

Woman That is symbolism, surely? What do you know of symbols? Are you trained? Are you one of these new educated women?

Mina Ask Jonathan. He used to introduce me as his little typist in those days. Anyway, I was a girl, a woman, just like Lucy. When she died they decided I must be kept from harm. *(Ironic)* Just like her.

Woman *(missing the irony)* So they isolated you? While they took up the search? They put you in a place of safety?

Mina Indeed they did. A madhouse where I was alone with Mr Renfield, Dracula's amanuensis*, next door to Carfax, the house and chapel where Dracula's coffins lay, where he spent his resting hours. Next door! To quote the great Professor once again: I had a man's brain. I should hope not, doctor. I should hope not.

---

* person employed to take instructions

Woman You must not blame too harshly, Mrs Harker. It was all done for the best, I'm sure.

Mina Isn't that what doctors always say? They left me all alone with one mad person, with another roaming round outside. At the very least they might have guessed that Renfield would let his master in. He did. John Seward, in another stroke of masculine intelligence, very kindly gave me a drug to render me unconscious, and Renfield called his master in to feast.

Woman *(consulting notes)* But was your husband not there with you, on that night? October 3rd, was it? Did he not sleep with you? At your side?

Mina He did. He was. He slept like a new-born babe when he finally came home. He did not wake me up, I was too drugged. But Dracula came later. He woke me. Oh yes, indeed he did.

Woman And your husband lay beside you while this monster ... what?

Mina He sucked my blood. He bit my neck and sucked the life-blood out of me. And then he made me suck his own. And Jonathan slept beside me! He did not wake! He can not even remember that it happened! My protector! My man! My husband! I sometimes think that all the men in this – are *mad*!

***Woman** stands.*

Woman And you, I'm sad to say, are showing signs of paranoia, Mrs Harker. Unlike poor Lucy Westenra, you had at least been warned.

Mina Renfield tried to warn me. When he took his leave of me he kissed my hand most tenderly. *(Pause)* Then called in Dracula.

Woman Renfield paid the price. He is dead. When Van Helsing heard what he had done, his rage was incandescent*.

Mina Renfield tried to warn me.

Woman Renfield paid the price.

---

* red-hot

She walks out. ***Mina****, half following, throws herself instead onto the couch. After a brief pause,* ***Renfield*** *is brought in by* ***Seward*** *and* ***Van Helsing****, with* ***Harker, Godalming*** *and* ***Morris****. They surround his seat.*

Van Helsing *(accusatory)* So now we know it all, don't we? *You* brought him in! You let the monster in with poor dear Madam Mina!

Harker *(brokenly)* My wife. My darling little wife.

Morris He sent a plague of rats next door so we would be distracted!

Godalming We were decoyed from her side. That isn't British!

Renfield What's Britain got to do with it? He's from the East, don't you understand that yet? The plague is from the East! The life force, wild, exciting! From Turkey, Russia, the Slavic masses, Serbia, Croatia, Kosovo, the Muslim world. Virility! The downfall of the West!

Godalming What plague? There is no plague.

Renfield The Master's moving West. From the Balkans westward, infecting as he goes. Europe, Holland, England. And into America, that land of opportunity.

Morris He'll never get there. The US is the land of freedom. This Dracula's a beast, a monster. He won't get in.

Renfield Infect the women, and the men must fall. You wished to marry Lucy Westenra. All of you! There will be others that the Count has shared blood with.

Godalming Oh my God! Disgusting, so disgusting!

Harker *(to* ***Mina****)* Oh my dear, my dearest. What have you done?

Mina What have *I* done? Jonathan, you *drugged* me! Then you stayed asleep!

Renfield He'll meet, seduce, infect, destroy! In Transylvania there was no challenge any more, the brides are there and willing. In England they were waiting, and two have fallen now, the fight was hardly difficult. And then America. The Brave New World.

Harker *(to **Seward**)* Oh God, John, you said it to me! 'If America can go on breeding men like Quincey Morris, she will be a power in the world indeed!' And Quincey Morris – Lucy –

Morris I never did! I only ever kissed her once! John, you must believe me. And forgive.

Renfield He is the source! Count Dracula! Blood is the infector, woman is the carrier! It is unstoppable! Now Madam Mina –

Van Helsing *(roaring)* How dare you, sir! Stop up your filthy mouth! Attendants! Here! This instant!

*The **attendants** seize **Renfield** and hustle him out.*

Van Helsing *(following)* Come, gentlemen. This must be settled, once for all! We must end this moral filthiness!

***Harker** hangs back.*

Seward Jonathan?

Harker My job is to protect my wife.

Seward So be it.

*They leave. **Harker** tries to embrace **Mina**, who shakes him off.*

Mina *(sadly)* Why did you not protect me, Jonathan? Why did you let them drug me while you all went off?

Harker The sleeping draught was for the best, my dear. Medical advice.

Mina I didn't have a chance. I was incapable.

Harker You needed to catch up. Your nights had been atrocious. And when I came to bed nothing had happened, you must admit it. You were fast asleep. I swear it. You were sleeping like a baby.

The lights are going down.

Mina At least I woke up when the monster came. You did not, Jonathan. What had you taken? Too much brandy? I tried, but could not wake you. I was terrified.

He lies beside her. She flounces to lie on her side, facing away from him.

Harker We had been fighting rats. A plague of them in Carfax. We destroyed some of his coffins.

Mina And then there was a man. Tall and thin and all in black. Parted red lips, with sharp white teeth between. The red eyes I had seemed to see in the graveyard up at Whitby. I would have screamed, but I was paralysed. You lay beside me, like a corpse.

As she has spoken, ***Dracula*** *has appeared, moving slowly towards them on the bed, his face almost obscured in his cloak.*

Dracula If you make a sound, young woman, I shall dash his brains out before your very eyes.

Mina I could not move. I was bewildered. I could not speak or move.

Dracula First, some small refreshment to reward me.

He crouches beside her and bares her neck, leaning into it.

Dracula It will not be the last time, dearest, that your veins will slake my thirst.

Mina Oh God, pity me. He placed his reeking lips upon my throat. My strength was fading. I was in a swoon.

He buries his face in her neck, low, so that we can see her face still. Agony and ecstasy.

Mina How long this lasted, this horrible time, I do not know. Next time I saw his mouth, it was filled with blood. My blood.

He straightens up, and speaks to her.

DRACULA And you, their best beloved one, are now to me. Flesh of my flesh, blood of my blood, kin of my kin. And soon your husband will partake of you. And all those other men who find you irresistible, it will become their fate. You will take them, you will feed them, you will spread your knowledge and my strength! They, like you, will yet be mine, my creatures and my jackals!

He pulls back his cloak and bares his chest, which he rips bloodily with his clawed hand. He seizes her behind the head and thrusts her face against him, almost suffocating her. She struggles, but cannot escape.

DRACULA When my brain says 'come' to you, you shall come. Cross land or sea to do my bidding, you must hear my call. For you have slaked your thirst on me. You have shared my appetite.

He pulls her bloodstained face away from him, drops her back onto the bed, and sweeps up and out. ***Mina*** *lies there, exhausted and in agony.*

MINA Oh God, oh God, what have I done? Unclean, unclean! God pity me!

She sits up and begins to rub her lips, frantically. Lights cut to black. Then out of the darkness, from offstage, a heart-rending, appalling scream, suddenly cut off. Flash lights to full. ***Van Helsing*** *is at the back, arms spread out, full of bonhomie*. In his hand is* ***Renfield's*** *straitjacket, and on his lips a smile.*

VAN HELSING Madam Mina. Jonathan. A tragedy. Poor Renfield has been murdered.

Behind and past him ***Seward, Godalming*** *and* ***Morris*** *pour on, as* ***Harker*** *springs to his feet, off the bed.*

HARKER Murdered? But who?

SEWARD Not suicide? I predicted suicide.

GODALMING He had it coming to him! A common bounder!

---

* extreme friendliness

Van Helsing It was, I fear, Count Dracula.

Mina He's come for me! He will reclaim me!

Morris We must get guns!

Van Helsing He has gone. I saw a bat rise from Renfield's window, and flap westward.

Godalming Carfax! We can kill him in his lair!

Van Helsing The opposite direction. He must have other coffin-loads of earth. Our job is now to track them down. Destroy them. Gentlemen, dear lady, it will not be easy, but we will surely win. Dracula! Your time is almost nigh.

Fade to black.

Scene Twelve

The space is divided into areas separable by lighting cues. At the back are dimly seen three white shrouds, laid out like beds, side by side. At the desk is ***Seward****, with* ***Godalming****,* ***Morris*** *and* ***Harker*** *facing him. A conference.*

Seward Tell it me again. The details must be absolutely accurate, the smallest error, now, is fatal. How many boxes of unholy earth were left to him? How many did he bring to Whitby in the first place?

Morris Sixty. But when he fled from London Docks there was just one, the one he lay in for the journey back by sea. We had destroyed the rest.

Godalming We bribed the carriers for the addresses where he'd hidden them. We tracked them down in Whitby, Carfax, Piccadilly ... and those rather awful London places.

Harker Bermondsey. Mile End.

Godalming One could tell he was not *English* aristocracy. Imagine if our dear Queen had met him!

Morris *(chiding)* Hush, Arthur! This is important work, stick to the details. Jonathan tried to kill him at the Piccadilly house when he rushed at us. *(To* ***Harker****)* Good try, my friend, good try!

Harker I only tore his coat with the knife-blade, he was too fast for me.

Morris You're too modest. You made him drop his gold and banknotes. You hindered him.

Harker He got away. He mocked us. 'My revenge is just begun,' he said. The words are etched forever on my heart. 'I spread it over centuries, and time is on my side. The girls that you all love are mine already, and through them you shall also all be mine.' And when Van Helsing touched Mina with the holy wafer, to comfort her – it burnt her face. Indelibly. She was lost. All of us were lost.

SEWARD No! Mina fought! She would not give up the struggle. She realised that in hypnosis she was linked to Dracula, she was near to him, and she endured all those sessions till we traced him to the ship in London Docks. The *Czarina Catherine*, Black Sea bound, for Varna.

HARKER We traced the ship and then we lost it. She'd already sailed. And all the while Mina was changing, what use in denying it? Her teeth were sharper, her eyes were hard. She began to treat me ... monstrously.

GODALMING Come, come! No way to talk about a lady!

HARKER She warned me I could no longer trust her. We could tell her nothing of our plans. She would betray us.

SEWARD Because Dracula could read her mind as well! Be fair!

MORRIS She also made us promise we would kill her if she changed too much. If that was monstrous, it was monstrous bravery.

HARKER To drive a stake into her heart and cut off her head. God help me, she was revelling in the thought of her own blood!

SEWARD And you are raving, Jonathan. The strain has been too great for you. Stick to the facts. We found the ship had sailed, we booked ourselves on trains to Transylvania, we stocked up with gear and rifles, and we came up with a plan.

MORRIS We found out where he'd landed, and his scheme of going up by river till he'd nearly reached his castle, lying in a coffin full of earth. They were Winchesters, as well. Repeaters, the very finest gun!

GODALMING Jonathan, no group of people could have done it better. You and I in a steam launch pursuing up the river, Jack Seward there and Quincey – and his precious guns! – on horseback in case, somehow, the Count gave us the slip.

SEWARD And Mina and Van Helsing up the Pass by carriage with the equipment to purify whatever filth they found at Castle Dracula.

GODALMING Holy wafers, crucifixes, wooden stakes, *et cetera*.

Harker Why Mina, though? How was she safe? To be sent into the jaws of hell tainted with the Devil's illness! To go into his death-trap! Infamy!

Seward It was explained. Without her Van Helsing might have missed the Count. He needed her hypnotic power to track him with the utmost accuracy. If he had escaped us this time he could have lain dormant for a century. More. And *then* Mina would have been called to him, her soul lost to God forever. It was *necessary.*

Godalming And she did save Van Helsing's life. High in the Borgo Pass after our launch was wrecked and his coffin had already been loaded on a leiter-waggon by his gipsy guards. Van Helsing put her in a holy ring but the women came to them. Had they seduced him … then all of us … the world … were lost …

During this, ***Van Helsing*** *and* ***Mina*** *have been trudging on, travel-weary and exhausted. She has sat down and he has made a circle round her with broken wafer, then built a fire. The three* ***female vampires*** *move silently onstage. One fair-haired and two dark. The lighting changes.*

71

Van Helsing Madam Mina. You must eat. You are paler than the snow.

Mina *(inside the circle)* I do not hunger. Not for food.

Van Helsing This circle is of the sacred wafer. But leave it for a moment. Come to me, here. Come to the fire.

The ***women****, moving catlike inwards, react.* ***Mina*** *stands, but she is weak.*

Van Helsing Will you not come? It is warmer here.

She steps to the edge of the circle, then stops.

Van Helsing Why not go on?

Mina *(simply)* I cannot cross.

Van Helsing Then I rejoice.

*The **women** dart up eagerly, but they can't break through.*

VAMP ONE Come, sister! Come to us! Come! Come!

VAMP TWO You are of the sisterhood, you have lain with him.

FAIR GIRL Dracula has enfolded you. You have drunk his blood.

VAMP ONE Come with us. The Master is returning.

VAMP TWO We have made a marriage bed.

FAIR GIRL It is getting light. Come with us now, for time is short. Oh sister, come! Soon he'll be here.

VAMP ONE The Master!

VAMP TWO Dracula. Our lord.

*They start to move away, imploring with their gestures. **Mina** stays. But suddenly, as if tortured, **Van Helsing** begins to follow.*

MINA No, no! Do not go with them, Van Helsing! Don't go!

*The **vampires** go to their tombs and lie down. Only their faces are showing. The outer two become still, but the **fair girl** holds up her arms, enticing **Van Helsing**. Tombs in dim, dim light.*

VAN HELSING *(in a dream)* So beautiful. So languorous. So voluptuous.

FAIR GIRL My face is fair, my heart is open. Man is weak.

VAN HELSING Those lips. That mouth, those eyes exquisite. It is man's instinct.

FAIR GIRL Kiss me, then. For you are lost. Just one small kiss. My dear. Is all I crave.

VAN HELSING Sweet fascination.

*As he bends over her mouth, **Mina** moves to the very edge of the circle, trying to break out. As his lips seem to touch the **fair girl's**, **Mina** half calls, half screams, very quietly. It is mournful, pitiful, keening, low. She is on her knees, arms upraised.*

MINA Van Helsing, no! There is poison in my blood. You are giving up our souls... to *hell*.

Suddenly it reaches **Van Helsing's** *brain and he is galvanized**. *He roars with horror and anger, and jerks hammer and stake from his bag. In a frenzy he penetrates the heart of the* **fair girl**, *throwing himself about so that all three are in a jumble. The air is full of awful screams and roars and hammering.* **Mina** *is on her knees, face in hands, when* **Van Helsing** *rushes down into the holy circle, seizes her arms, and hustles her to one side of the area, where they are almost hidden. Lights up on* **Harker** *and* **Godalming**, *who are apart from* **Seward** *and* **Morris.**

HARKER The accident to the launch was our blackest moment. We lost sight of the boat with its dreadful cargo and its band of fearsome gipsies. All we could do was get some horses, then follow on their tracks.

MORRIS *(light him and* **Seward***)* But me and you, Jack, we were luckier. As we rode down towards the river, we saw them race away, clustered round the leiter-waggon, as if beset. The howling of wolves. The falling snow. We knew we rode to death in some way. It was kind of depressing.

VAN HELSING *(loud)* Madam Mina! Look! Look!

She springs up and stares across the valley. Lights up on them.

VAN HELSING Mounted men! A leiter-waggon! It's gipsies of some sort!

MINA It's carrying a great square chest! It is the coffin! Van Helsing, it is the monster's coffin!

VAN HELSING They race the sunset! If they can stay away from us until the sun goes down – he will escape!

MINA They're coming straight towards us! What can we do? What can we do?

SEWARD And then we saw them, too. We swept around a corner from the south, and saw them, careering along.

---

* stimulated into action

Godalming Then us, then me and Jonathan! From the north side of the pass! It was a pincer movement! It was worthy of a Wellington or Marlborough*!

Mina They're coming for us! They're coming for our hiding place!

Van Helsing The sun is going down!

Godalming, Harker, Seward, Morris, Van Helsing *and* ***Mina*** *all rush suddenly towards the back. As they converge, the lights flash up then down again to very dim. There is much noise, a general melee. Knives, stakes, hammers are all brandished. Then a figure emerges.*

Harker *(screams, knife held aloft)* It is the Count! It is the Count! It is Count Dracula!

At the back, kicking through the winding sheets, comes **Dracula.** *Fully cloaked, face obscured, arms wide open, roaring. With a knife, he stabs* ***Morris*** *to the ground. Then* **Van Helsing** *jumps forward, and punches a stake towards his chest.* **Dracula** *stumbles backwards, crashes to the ground, where he is obscured by people and his robes.*

Van Helsing Then Dracula! Must die!

He bestrides the body, and hammers in the stake, with violence. Then he stands and faces forwards. He, too, looks like **Dracula** *once more. The others gaze at him.*

Van Helsing But we – mankind – are saved.

He stretches out his arms, and a triumphant tableau forms around him. As they hold it, the lights come up to full.

Then through the back comes the **woman doctor.** *She seems impatient.*

Woman *(acidly)* You. All of you. Get back down there. This is a consulting room, not a madhouse.

Mina Correction, doctor. It is a madhouse.

---

* British army leaders of outstanding ability

Woman Very amusing. You know precisely what I mean.

Seward *(looking at the recumbent form)* Quincey's dead.

Harker Of course he is. Dracula stabbed him, didn't he? The Borgo Pass, sixth of November, 1897.

Mina If we had a baby, Jonathan, we could call him Quincey, couldn't we? A sort of homage to our friend.

Godalming He'd never get to Eton, with a name like that. How *do* those Yankees do it?

Woman Now come on, everyone, the party's over, it's getting late. Back to your wards, please. Evening medication time. Renfield, on your feet.

*From under the pile of robes and sheets **Dracula** clambers up, and reveals himself as **Renfield**. He opens his small box.*

Renfield That was jolly good. Anyone for a juicy little spider? I've got some cockroaches.

Mina You're completely mad. Come on Quincey. Time for beddy-byes. Would you like to be my little baby boy?

***Quincey Morris** stands up.*

Morris Suits me, sister. What do babies get for tea? Apple pie and ice cream?

They are all leaving.

Woman Mince and mashed potatoes, just like yesterday.

Seward Just like every day. It gives me indigestion.

Woman Ah, well. Sweet dreams!

They've gone. Blackout.

Staging the play

Bram Stoker's *Dracula* is one of those stories, like Mary Shelley's *Frankenstein*, that everybody thinks they know, whether they have read it or not. Both writers, almost certainly, set out with the intention of investigating an idea, rather than creating a monster that would take on a life of its own. But that's what happened. Count Dracula and Baron Frankenstein's monster have been made into plays, films, cartoons, had other books and plays written about them – they are part of our heritage. They join a long list of other monsters: witches, werewolves and zombies, ghosts, mummies and giant gorillas. Monster-dramas are very difficult to stage seriously – too many Hollywood and Hammer horror films have seen to that. Men with bolts through their neck, or pointy fangs, are rarely frightening, and always unbelievable. Stoker in his original novel meant the threat of evil spreading throughout the world, feeding on the innocent, to be taken seriously.

This version of *Dracula*, with careful staging, can be chilling. Where the novel ranges over many different locations and images, Jan Needle's adaptation has pared these down to a stark, simple setting in a psychiatric hospital where even the owner, John Seward, sometimes wonders if he himself is mad.

SPACE

The play can be adapted to any performance space though you will need to think about a number of things when deciding how to stage it. Jan Needle does not say in his stage directions exactly where the play is set, though it is clearly a psychiatric hospital, or lunatic asylum as Stoker would have called it.

- What picture does that create in your mind? Make a list of adjectives to describe the setting. How can you convey that image simply but effectively?
- Does the setting have to be historically accurate?
- Which props and pieces of furniture do you need to stage the play? Make a list.

The play is an example of Gothic drama, a type of theatre characterized by gloomy surroundings, grotesque sights and supernatural events. Now think about the performance area where you are staging the play.

- What do you think are the particular problems posed by this kind of drama?
- How close do you want the audience to be? If the audience is too close to the drama, will it make them giggle with embarrassment, or is it more important to make the audience feel part of the action – almost as if they where fellow inmates of Dr Seward's asylum? If so, where will you seat them?
- If you double the characters in the play (see page 68), how and where will the actors change?
- Where will you keep the props, such as the straitjacket and the baby in the sack, so that they are a surprise when they are brought on?

Below are two possible set designs. Think about the advantages and disadvantages of each.

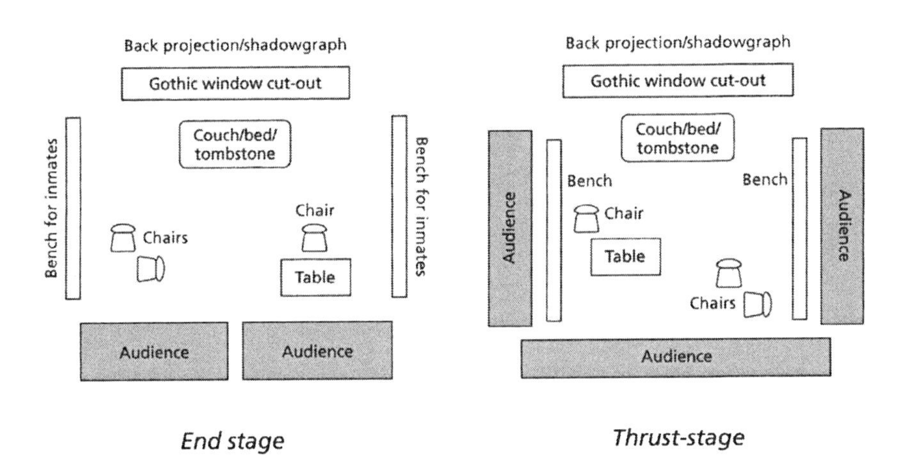

End stage

Thrust-stage

THE CAST

The play has 16 characters, with the parts of the attendants (non-speaking) and two of the vampires doubled. Some of the roles are very small, for example: Lucy's mother appears only once. Your group might be bigger or smaller than this. Turn this to your advantage.

Company too big?

Consider imaginative ways of using the company to set the scene: more inmates of the asylum, perhaps, or more vampires. You might want to look at some of the scenes from the book Jan Needle has left out and add them for your performance, for example:

- Jonathan Harker's encounter with the frightened peasants on his way to Count Dracula's castle
- the Whitby townsfolk talking about the shipwreck and the stories of the dead captain and the enormous dog
- a meeting between some children and the undead Lucy in the cemetery.

Company too small?

Doubling, where actors play more than one part, can solve a problem, and can also suggest interesting ideas to the audience.

In groups

- *Go through the play and work out who is on stage in each scene, and which characters might be doubled.*
- *What interesting connections might be made by doubling: Mrs Westenra and a female vampire; the woman doctor and Lucy; Dracula and Van Helsing?*
- *What would be the effect of having female actors playing male roles or vice versa?*

COSTUME

Often the most effective approach to costume is to keep it simple. The novel and play are set in the 1890s, in late Victorian England and Europe. You might choose to try and recreate the clothes of the period as closely as your budget will allow. Women wore long skirts, high-necked blouses and shawls; men wore suits and high-collared shirts. Count Dracula will, of course, need a cloak. But you will also want to distinguish the characters in other ways: young from old, rich from poor.

Costume design

In pairs

A. Make a list of characters and what each of them is like. A good way of doing this is to ask: 'If this character was an animal, what kind of animal would they be?' or 'If this character was a colour, what type of colour would they be?' Think about colour. For example: what does red mean to you? Which character might wear red? Is it a dark red or bright scarlet?

B. Look at photographs and paintings from the period and see how different people dressed. Look for ways in which you can add simple items – brooches, cufflinks, scarves, aprons – to a basic costume, which would help the audience work out who a character is.

On your own Choose one of the characters and design a costume for them in keeping with their character and the period. Draw pictures of your design and make notes on how you would set about making or finding the costume.

You might want to take a different approach to costume. The play is not straightforward. We don't always know who is mad and who is sane, who is in charge, who is the vampire and who the vampire-hunter. Take Dr Seward, for example: he is the doctor in charge of the asylum at the beginning of the play, but he is being questioned by a young woman who from her clothing also seems to be a doctor. Why? Are the attendants nurses or patients? Van Helsing often looks like Dracula. Is Dracula yet another patient in the asylum?

5

To suggest this uncertainty, you might choose to dress the actors in neutral costume, so that they can switch roles very easily: from doctor to patient, vampire to victim, etc.

Discussion

As a class

- What ideas do you associate with the colour white? What would be the effect if you dressed all the characters in white?
- You might then add individual costume items to indicate character, for example: a cloak; a medical bag; a straitjacket; a lace shawl. What items would you use for each of the characters in the play?
- Is there any other colour that might work better – or in a different way – than white as your basic colour?

LIGHTING

How you use lighting will depend on your resources but startling effects can be achieved with imagination and very little equipment. The play is full of light and dark images. A sudden change from dark to light or vice versa can heighten the tension and give the audience a jolt. Go through the play and identify the key light and dark moments.

- How many special effect lights do you have available? If you only have one spotlight, how can you best use it?
- Shadows across the floor and even across people could add to the scary atmosphere of the piece. How might you place your lights to achieve maximum effect?
- Will you want to use projected images in your production, for example: to create the bat effect in Lucy's bedroom?

MUSIC AND SOUND EFFECTS

Creaking doors, horrible groans and the howling of wolves are probably best left to Hammer horror films. Sound effects and spooky music could achieve the opposite to the effect you are looking for – by making the audience laugh. If you do use them, make sure they achieve what you want them to. Properly used, music can greatly enhance the drama of *Dracula*. You might want to find recorded music for your production. Philip Feeney's music for the modern ballet *Dracula* is on CD, as is Wojciech Kilar's soundtrack for Francis Ford Coppola's film *Bram Stoker's Dracula*.

You may prefer to make your own live music. Improvise and see what happens. Experiment with a series of spooky, minor bass chords, a single high violin note, a wandering treble line of reedy voices, to underline the drama in different scenes.

Blood and fire

Blood and blood capsules can be great fun, but they can also be funny. If you want the blood in the play to look real and frightening you will have to experiment – and plan very carefully – to make sure you get the best effect. The golden rule is don't use too much. Leave it up to the audience's imagination. Suggestion goes a long way.

If you don't want to use blood capsules you will need to think about how you will achieve the illusion, or idea, of blood in the play. Red ribbon or string may be more dramatic, and easier to manage, than stage blood. Use your imagination.

The fire in Scene 12 needs to be carefully worked out. It can't be a real fire, of course, but could perhaps be achieved with a flickering light from floor level playing onto Mina's face.

For the weapons in the play, think about whether you want to mime hammers, stakes and knives, or use props. You can get stage knives with retractable blades from joke shops and theatrical suppliers. Remember though that these are not toys.

Poster Design

There have been some wonderful book-cover and poster designs for different versions of *Dracula*.

In groups

Look at the cover of the original paperback edition (1901) of *Dracula* and the poster for the Bela Lugosi film of 1931, below. Discuss the differences between the two designs. What characters have they chosen to use? How would you describe the image of Dracula in each picture? What other images and words have they used? What mood does each design convey to you?

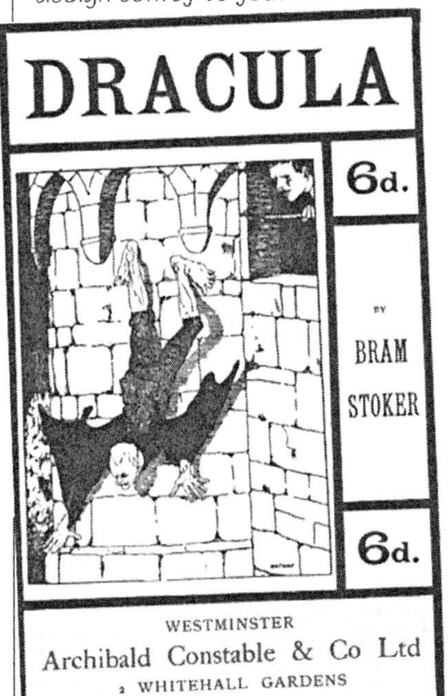

Cover of the original paperback edition of Dracula

Poster advertising the Bela Lugosi film of 1931

cont...

H

On your own

Design a poster for your production. Think carefully what atmosphere you want your poster to convey and how it can reflect this adaptation of *Dracula*. Look at other posters, advertisements or fonts on your computer and find the most effective images and lettering for your poster design.

This one is called Old English.

The life and times of Bram Stoker

Bram Stoker, theatre manager and writer of Dracula

Bram Stoker was born on 8 November, 1847 in Dublin, the third of seven children. His father was a civil servant. He was often ill as a child – until he was seven he was 'rarely on his feet'. He went on, however, to become university athletics champion and a capped footballer at Trinity College, Dublin where he studied Pure Mathematics (so much for that sickly childhood!). At the age of 22 he followed his father into the Civil Service as a clerk.

On August 28, 1867, however, he had an experience that was to change his life, when he saw the great and charismatic actor-manager Henry Irving, in Sheridan's *The Rivals*. He later described him as being 'as real as the person of one's dreams'. Stoker became an avid fan, and was later invited to dinner by Irving, after the actor read rave reviews of one of his performances, which Stoker had written. At the dinner,

Irving gave a recital of a poem which so affected Stoker that he fell into 'something like a violent fit of hysterics'. Whilst he was recovering, Irving brought him a photograph of himself, on which he had written: 'My dear friend Stoker – God bless you! God bless you! Henry Irving.'

In 1878 Stoker gave up his safe but predictable job as Inspector of Petty Sessions and became Irving's business manager at the Lyceum Theatre in London. Just before he left Dublin, Stoker married the beautiful Florence Balcombe, but their honeymoon was postponed to fit in with Irving's work schedule. The Stokers had one child, Noel, who in later life accused Irving of having taken over Stoker's life and 'worn Bram out', just as Count Dracula takes over the life of everyone in the play and drains them of all energy.

Several of Irving's most popular roles were evil and troubled characters, such as the Fallen Angel, Mephistopheles, in *Faust*, and the murderer, Mathias, in *The Bells*. Irving's own character and the roles he played are supposed to have been one model for the figure of Count Dracula.

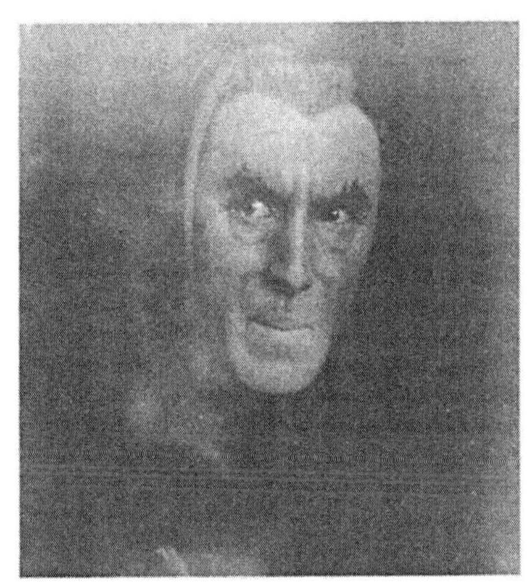

Irving as Mephistopheles in Faust

Bram Stoker's first horror story was published in 1875. *Dracula* was published in 1897 and became a best seller within a very short time. Stoker continued to work for Irving, who was knighted in 1895, until Irving's sudden death in 1905. On news of the death Stoker had a stroke and lay unconscious for twenty-four hours – the final proof of the hold Irving had over him? Stoker continued to write, and perhaps his second greatest tale, *The Lair of the White Worm*, was published the year before his own death in 1912.

Writing

On your own

A. Henry Irving was the greatest star of his day. Which present-day celebrity would you like to work for? Would you be prepared to devote your life to them as Stoker did to Irving? Write a short monologue in which you describe the moment at which you fell under the spell of your chosen star.

B. Stoker may have drawn upon the character of Irving when he created Count Dracula. Authors often do this. One of Jan Needle's early books, *Albeson and the Germans*, was based on his own childhood and the people he knew. Choose someone you know well, and write down a list of their characteristics. Change their name and sex. Using this new character as your hero, write a short story set either some time in the past or 100 years in the future.

cont...

c. In 1882 Bram Stoker was crossing the Thames in a ferry when a man leapt into the water in order to commit suicide. Stoker stripped off his coat and dived into the water and rescued him, though the man later died. He was awarded a bronze medal for his heroism. Irving is reported to have said: 'Bravo, Stoker! We pretend to be heroes on stage, but you really *are* one!'

From The Penny Illustrated, *November 4, 1882*

Stoker never wrote this story of his own gallantry. Which do you think pleased him more, the medal or Irving's praise? Write an account of the episode, either: an entry in Stoker's private diary; an account written by an eye-witness; a letter from one of Stoker's friends to another.

The Brave Bram Stoker

On your own The Victorians were very fond of melodramatic and sentimental songs, which often told stories of heroic bravery, the suffering of innocents, or the punishment of wickedness. Write the lyrics of a song entitled 'The Brave Bram Stoker', which tells the tale of Stoker's rescue of the drowning man in the most dramatic and colourful terms you can find. The song will need a rousing chorus with simple lyrics which are easy to remember.

In groups Devise a tune for one of the lyrics you have written. Perform the song as a group with suitable movements and gestures.

Work on and around the script

ADAPTING THE NOVEL FOR THE STAGE

Jan Needle writes: 'Stoker's novel is written in the form of letters, medical reports, newspaper stories and diary entries – which means that every incident is written from a different person's point of view, and every bit of action, however exciting, ends up as a report of action not the real thing. I chose to set this version in a hospital so that, like in the novel, we see these events and people from a distance, without getting too involved.'

Read the following extract from the novel, written from Jonathan Harker's point of view, during his stay at Castle Dracula.

From *Jonathan Harker's journal*, May 8.

I only slept a few hours when I went to bed, and feeling that I could not sleep any more, got up. I had hung my shaving glass by the window, and was just beginning to shave. Suddenly I felt a hand on my shoulder, and heard the Count's voice saying to me, 'Good morning.' I started, for it amazed me that I had not seen him, since the reflection of the glass covered the whole room behind me. In starting I had cut myself slightly, but did not notice it at the moment. Having answered the Count's salutation, I turned to the glass again to see how I had been mistaken. This time there could be no error, for the man was close to me, and I could see him over my shoulder. But there was no reflection of him in the mirror! The whole room behind me was displayed; but there was no sign of a man in it, except myself. This was startling, and, coming on top of so many strange things, was beginning to increase that vague feeling of uneasiness which I always have when the Count is near; but at that instant I saw that the cut had bled a little, and the blood was trickling over my chin. I laid down the razor, turning as I did so half round to look for some sticking plaster. When the Count saw my face, his eyes blazed with a sort of demoniac fury, and he suddenly made a grab at my throat. I drew away, and his hand touched the string of beads which held the crucifix. It made an instant change in him, for the fury passed so quickly that I could hardly believe that it was ever there.

'Take care,' he said, 'take care how you cut yourself. It is more dangerous than you think in this country.' Then seizing the shaving glass, he went on: 'And this is the wretched thing that has done the mischief. It is a foul bauble of man's vanity. Away with it!' and opening the heavy window with one wrench of his terrible hand, he flung out the glass, which shattered into a thousand pieces on the stones of the courtyard far below. Then he withdrew without a word. It is very annoying, for I do not see how I am to shave.

Writing and Drama 

On your own Write a stage version of this scene. You can use any of the dialogue in the extract or change it, but also write additional lines to complete the scene. Include some stage directions for the actors. Think carefully about the characterisation as well as the dramatic action. What does Jonathan's closing remark in the extract tell you about his character and his response to the encounter?

In pairs Choose one of your versions of the scene and rehearse it, then perform the scene to the rest of the class.

As a class Discuss the different versions of the scene you have watched, and decide which ones you think are most effective, and why.

Read the following extract from the novel, which describes strange events in Hampstead, after Mina has been ensnared by Count Dracula.

The Westminster Gazette, 25 September

A Hampstead Mystery

The neighbourhood of Hampstead is just at present exercised with a series of events which seem to run on lines parallel to those of what is known to the writers of headlines as 'The Kensington Horror', or 'The Stabbing Woman', or 'The Woman in Black'.

During the past two or three days several cases have occurred of young children straying from home or neglecting to return home from their playing on the Heath. In all cases the children were too young to give a properly intelligible account of themselves, but the consensus of their excuses is that they had been with a 'bloofer lady'. It has always been late in the evening when they have been missed, and on two occasions the children have not been found until early in the following morning … a correspondent writes us that to see some of the tiny tots pretending to be the 'bloofer lady' is supremely funny. … There is, however, possibly a serious side to the question, for some of the children, indeed all who have been missed at night, have been slightly torn and wounded in the throat. The wounds seem such as might be made by a rat or small dog, although of not much importance individually, would tend to show that whatever animal inflicts them, has a system or method of their own.

Another Child Injured

The Bloofer Lady

We have just received intelligence that another child missed last night, was only discovered late in the morning under a furze bush on the Shooter's Hill side of Hampstead Heath, which is, perhaps, less frequented than the other parts. It had the same tiny wound as has been noted in other cases. It was terribly weak, and looked quite emaciated. It too, when partially restored, had the common story to tell of being lured away by the 'bloofer lady'.

TV adaptation

H

On your own Write a scene for a television adaptation of *Dracula*, based on one of the events described above. Decide what the scene will show: a child's encounter with the 'bloofer lady' or the scene when the child is found after meeting her. Think of the scene as a series of camera shots from different angles and distances and decide what the viewers will see in each part of the scene. Does the camera zoom in on a character's face (close-up) or take in the whole scene (panorama)? Does the camera move or stay still? First write directions which describe in detail the location where the scene takes place. Then write the scene, including the characters' dialogue and directions describing all the different camera shots.

Jan Needle has converted the diaries, letters and medical reports of the original novel into a continuous drama. The scenes are not always in the order in which the events happened. One useful way of following the characters through the play would be to return the play to diary and letter form.

H

Writing

On your own

A. Write a brief summary of the events of the play, putting the plot in chronological order (the order in which the events took place). Now write one character's account of the story as a diary, or as a series of letters.

B. Mina and Jonathan often disagree in their versions of the events. Following the play, write the journal entries for each, giving their differing views.

C. Mina is often angry in the play at the way the men have treated her. They are very much men of the Victorian period who thought women feeble and inferior creatures who needed protection. The most flattering thing Van Helsing can say about Mina is that she has 'a man's brain'. Write an exchange of letters between Mina and another emancipated, 'new woman' friend, in which she tells her story and confides her frustration at the way she has been treated.

D. One important figure whose story we don't hear is Lucy's mother, yet it is she who, unwittingly, is responsible for Lucy's death. Tell her story either through a diary or a series of letters to a friend.

One of the things that makes the play of *Dracula* so frightening is the way that Count Dracula's evil gradually infects and destroys the characters' ordinary lives. Jonathan sets out innocently as a lawyer to sell a house, and is imprisoned by a vampire. Lucy and Mina, like any two young girls, discuss their boyfriends, then first Lucy, and then Mina, are attacked. A doctor, trained to save lives, ends up destroying life with a hammer and stake. Ordinary people end up in a madhouse.

Drama

In groups Set up an everyday scene, such as breakfast time before school, a family at the supermarket, friends gossiping outside the school gates. Then introduce a stranger whose aim is to persuade one or more of the characters present to leave their friends or family and join him or her in a mysterious, possibly evil scheme.

In pairs Devise a short scene in which one person plays an estate agent and the other plays a modern-day Count Dracula who wants to buy a house in an area you know well.

Play each of these scenes first as comedy and then as serious drama.

In pairs Choose one of the scenes with two characters from the play, for example: the scene between Lucy and Mina at Whitby. Devise a modern-day version of the scene. Would they react to events in the same way?

31

Themes within and around the play

VAMPIRES

The myth of the Nosferatu or vampire is to be found in most cultures. The figure of the Undead, who rises from the grave at night and seeks out a victim to drink their blood, is found as far back as the ancient Greeks. Vampires, in legend, are drawn particularly to young female virgins and new-born babies. Sometimes the vampire takes the form of an animal – a dog, cat, bat or wolf. Once bitten the vampire's victim becomes a vampire in turn, thus spreading the evil that the vampire represents.

There have been many superstitions about how people become vampires. These include:

- smoking on holy days
- having been a wizard, or werewolf, during one's lifetime
- committing suicide
- committing perjury
- dying unbaptised
- dying by violence or drowning
- being born the seventh son or daughter
- being born with teeth.

The ancient Greeks had a series of curses that were supposed to turn the recipient into a vampire:

MAY THE GROUND NOT RECEIVE HIM!
MAY THE EARTH NOT CONSUME HIM!
MAY THE BLACK EARTH SPEW THEE UP!
MAY THY BODY NEVER DECAY!

Drama

In groups

A. Think up imaginative ways of becoming a vampire in the 21st century. Choose one of these new ways and improvise a scene in which a character becomes a vampire by inadvertently bringing the curse upon themselves. What happens next? How is the vampirism spread?

B. Two people play the parents of a new-born baby who fear that their child may be a vampire. Find a reason for their worry from the traditional list on page 82 – or think of one of your own. Two others in the group play the doting grandparents on their first visit to see the new baby.

C. Create a short news item for the local television news on the vampire baby. How do you get across the facts? Who might you interview (the parents? a vampire expert?) and what questions would you ask?

Writing

On your own

A. Write the vampire child story as a newspaper item. Include an eye-catching headline.

B. Compose a poem made up of vampire curses.

People used to protect themselves against vampires by putting thorns around the doors and windows, so that the creature would catch itself on the thorns and become entangled. Garlic and horseshoes were also held to have protective powers. As creatures of the dark, vampires were believed to be allergic to light, and as creatures of the Devil they were repelled by crucifixes.

The traditional way of destroying a vampire was believed to be with a stake through the heart. A modern-day version is a silver bullet, blessed by a priest, fired through the coffin. Another traditional way was to stuff the mouth of the vampire with garlic and/or cut out the heart and burn it to ashes. Perhaps the most elaborate approach was recorded in Bulgaria, where whitethorn was placed in the navel of the vampire, the body shaved except for the head, the soles of the feet slit and a nail driven through the back of the head!

Real life vampires

The original Count Dracula seems to have been the historical figure of Vlad the Impaler or Vlad Dracul, who ruled Transylvania during the 5th century. He was known, not for drinking blood, but for spilling that of his enemies in the most hideous manner. His favourite method of punishing his victims was to impale them through whichever part of their body took his fancy, and watch them die slowly and horribly. Van Helsing rather mildly refers to him in the novel as 'no common man ... he was spoken of as the cleverest and most cunning, as well as the bravest of the sons of "the land beyond the forest" '.

Vlad the Impaler

There was also a historical female 'Dracula': the 17th century Hungarian Countess Elisabeth Bathory. Countess Bathory came to believe that drinking and bathing in the fresh blood of young virgins would guarantee her eternal life, and she is reputed to have killed thousands of young women to feed her obsession.

There was a well-documented outbreak of vampire hysteria in 1732 in which fourteen victims of an alleged vampire, a Hungarian soldier, Arnold Paole, were dug up and found to be in a 'vampiric state': their bodies still fresh, eyes filled with fresh blood, blood flowing from the ears and nose into the coffin. Their heads were cut off, their bodies burned and the ashes thrown into the River Moravia.

Media activities

In groups Imagine that you are modern-day reporters investigating a new discovery involving one of these historical figures. Create a one-minute news item for the Nine O'Clock News. You might want to include interviews with experts who can shed light on the story.

As a class Devise an imaginary chat show whose guests include Vlad the Impaler, Countess Bathory and Arnold Paole; OR an Oprah Winfrey-style 'confession' show in which the subject is 'I married a vampire'.

On your own Write up the historical vampire news story as two newspaper items, one for a tabloid newspaper and the other for a broadsheet. Think about what sort of angle each would take on the story, what headlines they might use, and how they would describe the people involved.

H

Stoker is supposed to have been inspired to write *Dracula* following a particularly grisly nightmare. Other writers have been inspired by dreams; some of Stoker's contemporaries were supposed to have induced nightmares by deliberately eating indigestible food at night, or stimulated waking dreams with drugs like laughing gas. Mary Shelley created her fabulous monster, Frankenstein, when one very long and stormy night, she and her friends set out to see who could write the best ghost story.

Discussion and writing

In groups

A. Discuss what dreams you have had that have really frightened you. Do your nightmares have recurrent themes or images? Do different people in the group have similar dreams? Do you dream in colour? What makes you feel safe after a nightmare?

B. Discuss what frightens you in real life. Is it the same thing or person that features in your nightmares? Are the people that scare you in your dreams ordinary people, or are they monsters like Dracula or Frankenstein?

C. Do you believe in ghosts? What are they? Have any of you seen a ghost?

cont...

D. Every society has its monsters. Why do we believe in these monsters, or have to invent them?

On your own

H

A. Write a short story or a poem inspired by the idea of nightmares, or based on a nightmare you have had.

B. Write a short story based on a real-life incident that scared you.

In groups Create your own ghost story, sitting in a circle. Choose a leader. One person starts a grisly ghost story (for example: 'One winter's night, Esmeralda was making her way back home through the churchyard ...') The leader decides when to interrupt the story and ask someone else to continue with it.

One of the most popular vampire stories before *Dracula* was a 'penny-dreadful' called *Varney the Vampire or the Feast of Blood* (1846). Like Dracula, the aristocratic vampire, Sir Francis Varney, preys on innocent young women. Unlike Dracula, his end comes when he leaps into the volcano, Mount Vesuvius. With a villain given to hissing and lurking round bone houses and cemeteries, Varney the Vampire seems to have more in common with the 20th-century comic cartoon figure, Count Duckula, than Stoker's terrifying Dracula. Count Duckula is a vegetarian, vampire duck with two faithful retainers, the lugubrious butler, Igor, and the foolish nanny, Nanny. The vampire hunter is called Von Goosewing.

The cover of Varney the Vampire

Count Duckula with Igor and Nanny

The female characters in *Dracula* are victims preyed on by men. In contrast, a modern-day version of the vampire myth has a female as its heroine: Buffy Summers.

Buffy the Vampire Slayer: *'Uninvited Guests'*

Discussion

As a class Compare the drawings of female characters on the cover of *Varney the Vampire* (1853) on page 86 and the extract from *Buffy the Vampire Slayer* (2000) on pages 87–88. How are the drawings different? Why do you think this is?

Cartoon Strip

On your own Create your own cartoon or comic strip based around a male or female vampire. It could be a version of *Dracula* or *Varney the Vampire*, or based around an entirely new character.

A. Write down the scenario for your comic strip. Draw a page in sketch form, including dialogue and captions.

B. Write down the scenario for one episode of your cartoon. Select one scene and write the script for that scene or take a scene from Jan Needle's adaptation of *Dracula*. Using a series of between ten and twenty frames, create a storyboard for that scene by drawing the sequence of action with dialogue.

BLOOD

Blood is the stuff of life. We each have about five litres of it in our bodies. However, blood can also kill. Given the wrong blood group you can die. Blood can also carry fatal diseases like malaria or HIV.

There are many sayings and rituals that reflect the importance of blood, for example: 'Blood is thicker than water' or the ritual of blood-brothers, in which blood is mixed as a symbol of friendship.

Discussion

In groups How many sayings or phrases can you think of that include the word 'blood'? What different things can blood symbolise?

One of the most powerful images of blood occurs in Shakespeare's play *Macbeth*, where the bloody hands of Macbeth and Lady Macbeth become both literal and metaphorical signs of their guilt. Immediately after Macbeth has killed his master the king, Duncan, he looks at his bloody hands and cries out:

What hands are here! Ha! They pluck out mine eyes.
Will all great Neptune's ocean wash this blood
Clean from my hand? No; this my hand will rather
The multitudinous seas incarnadine*,
Making the green one red.

Act 2, Scene 2

Later in the play, Lady Macbeth is driven mad by her guilt, and it is the blood on her hands that obsesses her even in her sleep. In this scene (Act 5, Scene 1), as she sleepwalks, symbolically washing the blood from her hands, she is observed by the doctor and her waiting gentlewoman.

Enter Lady Macbeth, with a taper.

Gentlewoman Lo you! Here she comes. This is her very guise; and, upon my life, fast asleep. Observe her; stand close.

Doctor How came she by that light?

Gent. Why, it has stood by her: she has light by her continually; 'tis her command.

Doctor You see, her eyes are open.

Gent. Ay, but their sense is shut.

Doctor What is it she does now? Look, how she rubs her hands.

Gent. It is an accustomed action with her, to seem thus washing her hands. I have known her continue in this a quarter of an hour.

Lady Macbeth Yet here's a spot.

Doctor Hark! she speaks. I will set down what comes from her, to satisfy my remembrance the more strongly.

Lady Macbeth Out, damned spot! Out, I say! One; two; why then 'tis time to do't. Hell is murky! Fie, my Lord, fie! A soldier and afeard? … Yet who would have thought the old man to have had so much blood in him?

Doctor Do you mark that? …

Lady Macbeth … What, will these hands ne'er be clean? No more o'that my lord, no more o'that; you mar all with this starting.

Doctor Go to, go to; you have known what you should not.

* to stain or tinge with red

GENT. She has spoken what she should not, I am sure of that. Heaven knows what she has known.

LADY MACBETH Here's the smell of blood still. All the perfumes of Arabia will not sweeten this little hand. Oh! Oh! Oh!

DOCTOR What a sigh is there! The heart is sorely charged. … This disease is beyond my practice. Yet I have known those which have walk'd in their sleep who have died holily in their beds.

LADY MACBETH Wash your hands, put on your night-gown; look not so pale. I tell you again, Banquo's buried; he cannot come out on's grave.

DOCTOR Even so?

LADY MACBETH To bed, to bed: there's knocking at the gate. Come, come, come, come, give me your hand. What's done cannot be undone. To bed, to bed, to bed.

Macbeth has many themes in common with *Dracula*. They both deal with the supernatural, sleepwalking and madness. Macbeth is driven on in his ambition by the three witches and haunted by the ghost of his murdered friend, Banquo. Lady Macbeth sleepwalks and in the end goes mad and kills herself.

In groups Write a script for a modern English version of the sleepwalking scene with a modern setting. Use a dictionary and an annotated copy of the play to help you. Complete the scene between the Doctor and the Gentlewoman. What might they do with their knowledge of Lady Macbeth's guilt? Rehearse and perform the scene in front of the rest of the class.

INFECTION

Dracula drinks blood. When he does so he 'infects' his victims with vampirism. They, in turn, infect others. Nineteenth-century Britain suffered many outbreaks of infectious diseases, whose causes were not fully understood. One possible source for some of the more gruesome details in the novel *Dracula* may be Bram Stoker's mother's own account of a nineteenth-century epidemic.

Cholera outbreak

Charlotte Stoker, when she was a girl in Sligo in the west of Ireland, lived through an outbreak of cholera in 1832 that killed more than half the people in the little town. Nobody knew what caused the disease in those days (cholera is caught by drinking infected water), and people became very violent towards the ill, in case they passed the illness on. Charlotte Stoker wrote about it in a letter to her son in about 1875.

> One action I vividly remember. A poor traveller was taken ill on the roadside some miles from the town, and how did those samaritans tend him? They dug a pit and with long poles pushed him living into it, and covered him up quick, alive.

Another memory seems astonishingly close to the idea of the Undead, and of Count Dracula in his mighty coffin.

> There was a remarkable character in the town, a man of great stature, who had been a soldier and was usually known as Long Sergeant Callen. He took the cholera, was thought dead, and a coffin was brought ... too short. The men who were putting him in, when they found he would not fit, took a big hammer to break his legs and make him fit. The first blow roused the sergeant from his stupor, and he started up and recovered. I often saw the man afterwards.

Most interesting of all, given that Count Dracula spreads his 'plague' by a kind of kissing, is this extract from the letter:

> The world was shaken with the dread of a new and terrible plague. It was the cholera, which for the first time appeared in Western Europe. Its bitter strange kiss, and man's want of experience and knowledge of its nature, or how best to resist its attacks, added, if anything could, to its horrors.

The young Charlotte, with her family, was forced to flee the town. At one stage they had to be protected from angry attackers by the local troops. When they returned to Sligo, grass had grown in all the streets. But there were hardly any people left.

Typhoid Mary

Another deadly disease much feared in Europe in the 1890s, and still a threat in parts of the world today, particularly in the wake of natural disasters, was typhoid. Shortly after Stoker's novel was published, a strange case of a 'plague-carrier' was reported in the United States. A travelling cook called Mary Mallon was discovered to be carrying a deadly strain of typhoid. By the time it was discovered, she was reputed to have infected 53 of her customers, and five had died. Her 'victims', in turn, infected 1300 people before the epidemic was stopped.

Research and presentation

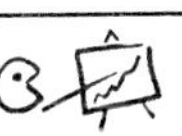

H

In groups Using your local library, and the internet, find out what you can about either cholera or typhoid. Prepare and give a short presentation on the history of the disease: past epidemics and the different treatments that were used; and on the disease itself: cause, symptoms, present-day treatment.

Writing

H

On your own

A. Imagine that you are a reporter at the time of either the cholera or typhoid outbreaks. Using the research you have done into one of the diseases, write a newspaper article with a suitably striking headline. Include interviews with eyewitnesses, relatives of the victims and scientific 'experts' of the period.

B. Imagine that you are Charlotte Stoker returning to her home town after the cholera outbreak. Write an account of her first days back in Sligo.

Research resources and further reading

BOOKS

Bram Stoker a biography by Barbara Belford (Phoenix Giant)
Classics of the Horror Film by William K. Everson (Citadel Press)

Dracula and vampire myths
Dracula by Glennis Byron (Macmillan Press)
Vampyres: Lord Byron to Count Dracula by Christopher Frayling (Faber and Faber)
Vampires by Bernhardt J. Hurwood (Quick Fox)
In Search of Dracula by Raymond McNally and Radu Florescu (Robson Books)
Countess Dracula by Tony Thorne (Bloomsbury)

Monster fiction
True Monster Stories by Terry Deary (Hippo Books)
Best Ghost Stories by Charles Dickens (Wordsworth Classics)
Collected Ghost Stories by M.R.James (Wordsworth Classics)
The Complete Tales and Poems of Edgar Allan Poe (Penguin)
Frankenstein by Mary Shelley (Penguin)
The Strange Case of Dr Jekyll and Mr Hyde by Robert Louis Stevenson (Penguin)
Dr Jekyll and Mr Hyde adapted by Simon Adorian (Collins Classics Plus)

FILMS

Hundreds of Dracula films have been made over the years. These are some of the best:
Nosferatu with Max Schreck, directed by Friedrich Wilhelm Murnau, 1921
Dracula with Bela Lugosi, directed by Tod Browning, 1931
Abbott and Costello Meet Frankenstein with Bela Lugosi as Dracula, 1948

The Horror of Dracula with Christopher Lee, Hammer, 1958
Taste the Blood of Dracula with Christopher Lee, Hammer, 1959
Dance of the Vampires directed by Roman Polanski, 1967
Nosferatu with Klaus Kinski, directed by Werner Herzog, 1978
Bram Stoker's Dracula with Gary Oldman, directed by Francis Ford Coppola, 1992
Buffy the Vampire Slayer with Kristy Swanson, directed by Fran Rubel Kuzui, 1992
Dracula: Dead and Loving It with Lesley Nielsen, directed by Mel Brooks, 1995
Count Duckula directed by Chris Randall

MUSIC

The Devil Rides Out by James Bernard (Silva Screen CD)
Dracula by Philip Feeney (Naxos CD)
Bram Stoker's Dracula original soundtrack by Wojciech Kilar (Soundtrax CD)
Horror! Monsters, Witches and Vampires (Silva Treasury CD)

Activities Mapping

English Framework Objectives (Year 7/8/9)

Page Number	Learning Objectives (Year 7/8/9)			
	Word (W) & Sentence (S) Level	Text Level		Speaking & Listening
		Reading	Writing	
66	**(7)** W17		**(7)** 2	
67				**(7)** 12, 13 **(8)** 10, 12 **(9)** 10
68		**(7)** 2, 4		**(7)** 12, 13 **(8)** 10 **(9)** 10
69		**(7)** 2, 4	**(7)** 3	**(7)** 12, 13 **(8)** 10, 13 **(9)** 10
70		**(7)** 2, 4		**(9)** 10
71				**(7)** 13 **(8)** 13
72			**(9)** 12	
75			**(7)** 5, 6, 7, 9, 14 **(8)** 5, 6	
76	**(7)** S15 **(8)** S12		**(7)** 3, 6, 9 **(8)** 5	**(7)** 16, 17 **(9)** 10

78		**(7)** 6	**(7)** 6, 9	**(7)** 11, 15, 16, 17, 18 **(8)** 14, 15, 16 **(9)** 12, 14
79		**(7)** 7	**(7)** 6, 7, 9, 11, 13, 14 **(8)** 10 **(9)** 5, 11	
80	**(7)** S15 **(8)** S12	**(7)** 6, 7	**(7)** 3, 6, 9 **(8)** 5, 7	
81				**(7)** 15, 16, 17, 18 **(8)** 14, 15, 16 **(9)** 12, 14
83	**(7)** S15, S17 **(8)** S9, S12 **(9)** S4, S9		**(7)** 6, 8, 9, 11, 12, 14 **(8)** 5, 7, 12 **(9)** 11, 12	**(7)** 15, 16, 17, 18 **(8)** 14, 15, 16 **(9)** 10, 12, 14
85	**(7)** S15, S17 **(8)** W12, S9, S12 **(9)** S4, S9		**(7)** 6, 9, 11, 12, 14 **(8)** 12 **(9)** 11, 12	**(7)** 3, 12, 13, 17 **(8)** 2, 10, 13, 15 **(9)** 3, 10
86			**(7)** 5, 6, 7, 8, 9 **(8)** 5, 6	**(7)** 12, 13 **(8)** 10, 13
89			**(7)** 3, 9	**(7)** 12, 13 **(8)** 10, 13
91	**(7)** W12, W15, W16 **(8)** W7, S13		**(7)** 6, 8, 9 **(8)** 7, 8	**(7)** 15, 16, 17, 18 **(8)** 14, 15, 16 **(9)** 10, 12, 14
93	**(7)** S15, S17 **(8)** W12, S9, S12 **(9)** S4, S9	**(7)** 1, 2, 4 **(8)** 2, 3	**(7)** 3, 6, 9, 11, 12, 14 **(8)** 12 **(9)** 11, 12	**(7)** 3 **(8)** 3, 4 **(9)** 2, 10

Collins Plays Plus Classics

Other titles in the **Collins** Plays Plus Classics and Plays Plus series that you might enjoy:

Lorna Doone

R. D. BLACKMORE (Adapted by Berlie Doherty)

Blackmore's classic tale of high adventure set in the south west of England during the turbulent time of Monmouth's rebellion in 1685.

Themes: Love; class; law

Cast: 28 characters (plus extras)

ISBN 0 00 330226 1

The Woman in White

WILKIE COLLINS (Adapted by Keith West)

Walter and Marian are determined to get to the bottom of the mystery surrounding the woman in white who haunts them, even if it costs them their lives.

Themes: Mental illness; marriage; love

Cast: 13 characters (plus extras)

ISBN 0 00 323077 5

The Mill on the Floss

GEORGE ELIOT (adapted by Sue Saunders)

Maggie is always in trouble with her family, but as she and her brother Tom discover when their family falls on hard times, blood is thicker than water. Eliot's classic tale adapted as a play for school use gives students the opportunity to enjoy this National Curriculum author.

Themes: Gender roles; disability; families; growing up; unemployment

Cast: 25 characters

ISBN 0 00 323076 6

Ruth

ELIZABETH GASKELL (adapted by Robert Leeson)

Ruth tells the moving story of the experiences of a single woman with an unplanned pregnancy in the 19th century. This adaptation provides a fascinating insight into Victorian attitudes towards single mothers and the social implications of births outside of marriage.
Themes: Single-parent families; unplanned pregnancies
Cast: 32 characters (plus extras)

ISBN 0 00 330225 3

Dr Jekyll and Mr Hyde

ROBERT LOUIS STEVENSON
(adapted by Simon Adorian)

Presented in the form of a TV documentary involving expert witnesses trying to get to the bottom of the mystery surrounding Dr Jekyll and Mr Hyde, this dramatisation of Stevenson's classic tale is ideal for use in schools.
Themes: Drugs; transformation; mental illness; the media
Cast: 19 characters (plus chorus)

ISBN 0 00 323078 3

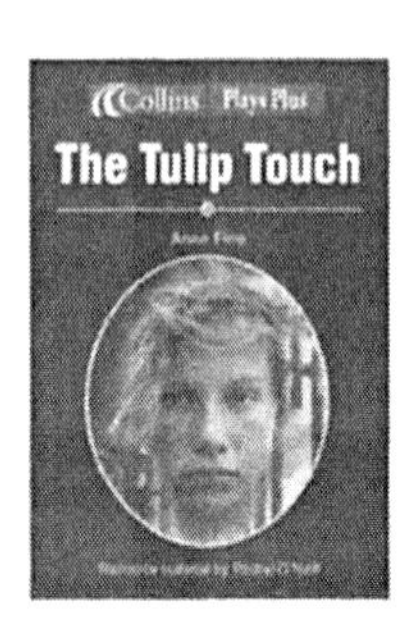

The Tulip Touch

ANNE FINE

A stunning adaptation by the author of the best-selling novel featuring the story of a disturbed teenager.
Themes: Juvenile crime; growing up and friendship
Cast: 22 characters (plus extras)

ISBN 0 00 713086 4

The Book of the Banshee

ANNE FINE

Adapted by Anne Fine from her popular novel, this is the story of teenage rebellion and its effects on a family.
Themes: Gender roles; family; growing up; pacifism and rebellion
Cast: 6 characters

ISBN 0 00 330310 1

Flour Babies

ANNE FINE

The amusing and moving adaptation of the novel exploring one boy's attempt to come to terms with his absent father through a school project on parenting.
Themes: Parenting; family
Cast: 19 characters

ISBN 0 00 330312 8

The Granny Project

ANNE FINE

When Ivan finds himself responsible for looking after his grandmother single-handedly he finds he has more than he had bargained for. The play is a humorous take on family roles and sensitively explores the issue of ageism.
Themes: Ageism; family roles; parenting
Cast: 7 characters

ISBN 0 00 330234 2

Street Child

BERLIE DOHERTY

Adapted from the award-winning book, *Street Child* is the story of the boy whose plight inspired Dr Barnardo to found his famous children's homes.
Themes: Homelessness; families
Cast: 55 characters (plus extras)

ISBN 0 00 330222 9

Mean to be Free

JOANNA HALPERT KRAUS

Set in America's deep south in the 19th century, this is the true story of Harriet Tubman, an ex-slave, who led slaves to freedom in Canada.
Themes: Slavery; freedom
Cast: 15 characters

ISBN 0 00 330240 7

The Thief

JAN NEEDLE

Focusing on a boy falsely accused of stealing, *The Thief* is a stimulating school-based drama.
Themes: Youth crime; self-deception; prejudice
Cast: 20 characters

ISBN 0 00 330237 7

The Bully

JAN NEEDLE

An adaptation of the best-selling novel that explores the unsentimental and realistic aspects of bullying and its impact in schools.
Themes: Bullying
Cast: 12 characters (plus extras)

ISBN 0 00 330227 X

The Birds Keep on Singing

STEPHEN COCKETT

The story of three evacuees billeted with two sisters during World War II. As the adults struggle to cope, the children come to a truce of their own.
Themes: War; relationships
Cast: 11 characters

ISBN 0 00 330315 2

In Holland Stands a House

SUE SAUNDERS

Based on the plight of Anne Frank who, with her family, went into hiding during the Nazi occupation. Drawing on her diary, the play skilfully interweaves domestic scenes from the annexe with wider events happening in Europe.
Themes: The Holocaust; racism; family; relationships
Cast: 11 characters (plus chorus)

ISBN 0 00 330242 3